Mrs. Pollifax has a beautiful new hat. Perfect for hiding 8 forged passports.

So it seems simple enough for her to deliver them to the Bulgarian underground, at the CIA's request. But when the prize-winning geranium grower from New Brunswick, N.J., is involved, nothing stays simple for very long. Mrs. Pollifax is trying to arrange a nice young man's escape from an escape-proof Bulgarian prison, with the aid of fireworks, a rope, a bow and arrow, stocking masks, and a gaggle of geese. All of which will earn Emily Pollifax many new fans, as well as delight those who have previously made her acquaintance.

The Elusive
Mrs. Pollifax

by
Dorothy Gilman

FAWCETT CREST • NEW YORK

The Elusive
Mrs. Pollifax

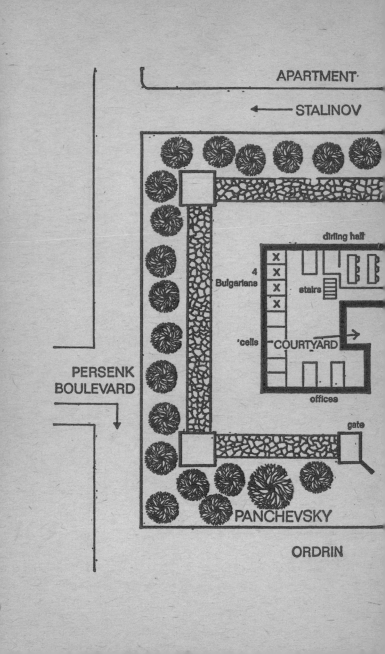

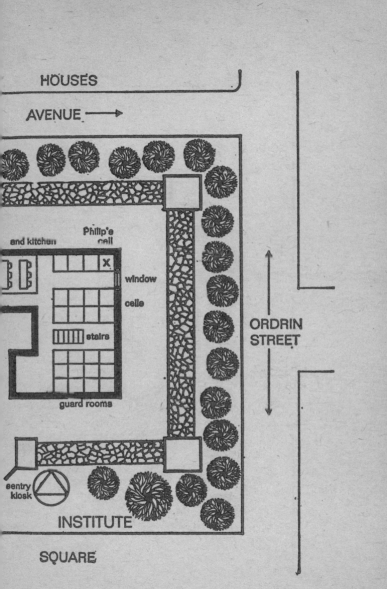

1

A small group of friends had assembled in Mrs. Pollifax's living room on this warm July evening. There was Miss Hartshorne from apartment 4-C across the hall; Professor Whitsun from the botany department of the university, and various loyal members of the Garden Club, led by Mrs. Otis, the president. For the last hour—without the slightest embarrassment—they had continued to check both their wristwatches and the clock on Mrs. Pollifax's wall. It was twenty minutes before midnight.

"Do you think *now*, Emily?" asked the president of the Garden Club anxiously.

"Yes, is it time?" asked Miss Hartshorne.

Mrs. Pollifax glanced at the professor for confirmation. He nodded. "Now or never I should say."

"Wonderful," breathed Mrs. Pollifax. "Lights out then, everyone!"

Flashlight in hand, she led the group into the kitchen. The window was open to the sultry night and the screen was already unlatched. Her flashlight played over the grillwork of the fire escape and came to rest on the box under the window. A reverent hush descended upon the group as they hung over Mrs. Pollifax's shoulder.

"It's bloomed," said Professor Whitsun in an awed voice. "I see it!"

"It's in bloom," called Mrs. Otis triumphantly over her shoulder to the others. "It's happened!"

"Turn on the lights and bring it inside," ordered Professor Whitsun. "Gently now. Are my cameras in place?"

Tenderly the window box was lifted to the sill, embraced and carried into the living room, where it was placed in the center of the rug.

"There are *three!*" cried Mrs. Pollifax, dropping to her knees beside a trio of delicate, spiky white flowers.

"So that's a night-blooming cereus," whispered Miss Hartshorne.

"They bloom just once a year, and then only for a few hours," said Professor Whitsun, adjusting the tripod for his camera.

"And Emily grew it on her fire escape," said Mrs. Otis. "Oh, Emily, it's *such* a coup for our Garden Club!"

"Speech," called the corresponding secretary.

"Yes, speech, Emily!"

"Hear! Hear!"

Beaming with pleasure Mrs. Pollifax rose to her feet and gently cleared her throat. "The night-blooming cereus . . ." she began.

At that same hour in New York City, Carstairs of the CIA and his assistant, Bishop, were sitting in a shabby Harlem hotel room under a single twenty-watt bulb suspended from the ceiling. The man they had come to see was slouched wearily on the edge of the unmade bed. His name was Shipkov, and he had just arrived from eastern Europe.

"I want the rest of this taken down in shorthand as well as taped," Carstairs told Bishop. To the man on the bed he added, "You're telling us that a stranger—a complete stranger—gave you accurate directions on just where and how to cross the Bulgarian border?"

The man nodded.

"Tell us again, slowly. Everything."

Shipkov closed his eyes in concentration. "It was in Sofia. I'd gone into a shop and he was waiting outside for me. He said 'Shipkov?' I turned. He began to speak to me in English—that was my first shock. He said, 'Your name is next on the List.' " Shipkov opened his eyes and made a face. "There is only one list in Bulgaria. It's not a healthy one."

"What did you say?" asked Carstairs, watching him closely.

Shipkov shrugged. "For how long have I lived in Sofia without a soul knowing I speak English? I was in shock. I can promise you it chilled the blood, a man calling me by name on the street and speaking to me in this language. I said nothing."

Carstairs nodded. "Go on."

"Next he told me, 'They're at your apartment now. If you go straight to Radzoi and cross the border at 11 P.M. tonight the border will be clear.' All I could think to reply was, 'Radzoi! That's the worst place of all to cross.' 'Not tonight,' he said. 'Not at eleven o'clock.' "

"Did he know you work for us?"

Shipkov laughed bleakly. "How can I even guess? The whole thing was wild."

"All right, go on."

"He said . . ." Shipkov closed his eyes, nodded and opened them. " '*If you make it across the border get us help. Some of us care, do you understand? Right now we desperately need passports, identity papers. The arrests grow insane.*' "

"And that's when he gave you the piece of paper with the address and the instructions?"

"Yes. And then he simply walked away down the street."

"Amazing," said Carstairs thoughtfully. "And you'd never seen him before in your life?"

"Never," vowed Shipkov.

"Describe him."

"An educated man, well dressed but shabby. About sixty. Definitely an intellectual. As you can see, the instructions are typed, so he had access to an English typewriter. I'd guess a professor, but how many professors know how to cross the border?"

Carstairs said slowly, "But you would trust this man?"

"I didn't then, I do now," Shipkov answered promptly. "I hurried back to my apartment, as I told you. The police had already arrived. Two men were running up the steps, one stood in my window shouting down to them. Needless to say I bolted."

"And you met no guards at all crossing the border at Radzoi?"

"Not a soul," said Shipkov. "It was like a miracle."

Carstairs exchanged glances with Bishop. "The kind of miracle we like to hear about," he said quietly.

"You want me to go back into Bulgaria with passports?" Shipkov asked. "With a new identity I could do it."

Carstairs shook his head. *"Much* too risky. This will need a courier—a particular kind of courier." He frowned. "Have you any idea how the police got on to you?"

Shipkov sighed. "Too many questions about General Ignatov, I think. I confess to some carelessness there. I got carried away. But something's definitely up."

Carstairs leaned forward. "You discovered more?"

Shipkov nodded. "The general's been courting some of the younger members of the secret police. The new ones, the hero-worshipers. I've seen them going into his house late at night when he's in Sofia. Enough to make up a small cadre of loyal supporters if his ambitions grow any bigger."

Carstairs whistled.

"A dangerous man," Shipkov said, nodding. "Ruthless.

A hero, too, after taking Bulgarian troops into Czechoslovakia in '68. The Soviets, they are very impressed with him."

"General Ignatov," mused Carstairs, and then with a glance at Shipkov he brought himself back to the moment. "You need rest, you look like hell," he said, and scrawling a few words on paper he added, "Go to this address, the people there will take care of you. On Tuesday I want to see you in Washington and we'll get the rest of this on tape." He drew bills from his pocket and handed them to Shipkov. "Get some clothes, too—and for God's sake be out of this place in an hour."

"Thanks," Shipkov said, pocketing money and papers. "Sorry I couldn't finish the job, Carstairs."

"Fortunes of war," Carstairs said, rising. "Bishop?"

Bishop finished locking the tape recorder. "Ready, sir."

With a nod to Shipkov they went out, descended dark, cluttered stairs and reached the street.

2

When they had walked several blocks in silence Bishop said, "Shall I call a cab now, sir?"

Carstairs shook his head. "No, I don't think we'll be heading back to Washington yet. Get us a car and driver instead, Bishop. I believe we'll take a little drive into New Jersey."

"At this hour?"

Hands in his pockets, brows drawn, Carstairs said, "That was a wild story Shipkov brought us."

"It certainly was."

"What's wildest of all, I buy it," Carstairs said thoughtfully. "Which leaves us with the possibility that some kind of Underground may actually be forming in Bulgaria. And if they need a few passports—"

"Then you need a courier," finished Bishop.

"Exactly." Carstairs turned his face to Bishop and smiled; there was a twinkle in his eye. "Any suggestions?"

Without change of expression Bishop said, "You asked me to remind you, sir, never to use her again. You said she breaks all the rules—doesn't even *know* there are rules—and you age ten years while she's on assignment. In a word, sir, she's too much of a worry to you."

"Nonsense," retorted Carstairs, "it'll be different this time."

"I believe you said that before, too," Bishop pointed out.

Carstairs stopped and glared at him. "Damn it, if I want Mrs. Pollifax, then I'm damn well going to get Mrs. Pollifax. That is, if she can leave her karate and her geraniums," he amended.

"She's not growing geraniums this season," Bishop told him. "I believe she's trying her hand at the night-blooming cereus."

"Good God," said Carstairs, and then he glanced sharply at his assistant. "And how the hell do you know that?"

Bishop grinned. "Oh, we keep in touch, sir. She sent a fruit cake at Christmas—it made several members of the staff quite tipsy. There was a card at Easter, and she sent a knitted muffler in May. My birthday, you know."

"Good lord," said Carstairs, shaken. "Well, get a car and a driver for us and let's go. . . . Night-blooming cereus!" he repeated, and shook his head.

The car was equipped with telephones, and before they had even crossed the New Jersey marshes Carstairs was issuing orders and setting queries in motion. For a few minutes Bishop listened and watched, still fascinated after years of working with the man. He knew that by dawn they would be back in Washington—Carstairs was ordering a helicopter now to meet them at the New Brunswick airport—and the whole operation would be neatly under way and stored between file covers. And in Washington, thought Bishop, there would probably be a new crisis waiting—he closed his eyes and slept.

"Blast," he heard Carstairs say, and unwillingly Bishop opened his eyes.

"These damn budget cuts, this fiendish economy drive,"

sputtered Carstairs. "I've cleared this with Upstairs, but damned if they don't announce that if I'm sending a courier into Bulgaria with nothing but passports then my courier can jolly well smuggle in a few other items."

"Like what?" asked Bishop drowsily.

"Who knows? Something for that remaining agent we've got in Sofia, whatsisname, chap with the geese—"

"Radev," murmured Bishop. "Assen Radev."

"I'll fight it. I'll blast them. I refuse to share my couriers."

"Mmm," mumbled Bishop sympathetically.

"If you're going to sleep, Bishop," Carstairs told him coldly, "then for heaven's sake sleep and get it done with. I'll give you ten minutes and then let's buckle down to some *real* work."

Like a drowning man—how did Carstairs manage it, he wondered—Bishop clutched his proffered ten minutes and slept.

At two o'clock in the morning they were seated in Mrs. Pollifax's living room in New Brunswick, New Jersey, and she was looking at them as if they had just presented her with the Holy Grail.

"But I'd be delighted—absolutely delighted—to go to Bulgaria," she said, beaming at them, her face radiant.

Her appearance had immediately revived Bishop. She was wearing a voluminous robe of black and white stripes. It looked like a tent; it had probably once *been* a tent because there was a definitely rakish Arab look about it.

"But what an extraordinary story your Mrs. Shipkov told!" She hesitated and looked at Carstairs reprovingly. "Should you have mentioned his name to me?"

Bishop grinned across the coffee table at his superior. "Yes, should you have?"

"It is not," said Carstairs pointedly, "his real name."

Mrs. Pollifax nodded. "I'm relieved. And will I travel under an assumed name, too?"

Carstairs shook his head. "No point in being unnecessarily devious. We'd like you to be a straightforward American tourist as usual. In fact this time you can make a public announcement to your friends and children that you'll be off to the Dalmatian coast, with a few days in Sofia. You'll have plenty of time to get ready because I'm scheduling you to leave in about ten days."

"Oh, how nice," said Mrs. Pollifax in a pleased voice. "You can't believe how frustrating it's been, nobody knowing where I go. Miss Hartshorne travels religiously on tours, and this year she's urging me to visit Turkey—"

Carstairs broke into a laugh. "Turkey!"

"Yes," said Mrs. Pollifax, nodding. "How can I possibly tell her I've seen more of it than she has! There's Albania, too. I am probably the only person in New Brunswick to have visited Albania—even if I *was* in shackles," she admitted, "but my lips are sealed." Abruptly she asked, "But why ten days? Why not sooner?"

"Arrangements," said Carstairs. "They'll have to go by the conventional route. A visa. Letters to Balkantourist outlining what you'd like to see during your five or six days in Sofia."

"Balkantourist?"

"Yes, it's the only travel agency in Bulgaria, and it's run by the government. It *is* the government. They'll arrange your itinerary, they'll arrange everything, as well as watch over you with vast benevolence."

"That's clever."

"Yes, and you must never forget that it's the government watching over you. In fact Balkantourist is going to be your biggest problem, and we'll have to think of something to deflect their interest. Happily, this is their peak tourist season. They've not many English-speaking guides as yet so we'll hope and pray they won't be able to assign you a full-time guide. We'll see what we can come up with. You'll find the people themselves extremely friendly—the country's no larger than Kansas—and warm and nonpolitical, too. But not the government, Mrs. Pollifax. *Not* the government."

"I'll remember that," she said, nodding.

"Now about the passports—"

"Yes," said Mrs. Pollifax, leaning forward eagerly.

"I've always had the impression that you wear hats everywhere except to bed—an illusion I prefer to cherish," he said with a glance at her uncovered head. "I think we'll put them in your hat."

"How inventive!" she said warmly.

"A special hat," he went on. "Custom-made, with a false crown. Two crowns, actually. I've already set this in motion. A chap named Osmonde will call on you to consult about the design. Will Thursday morning at ten be convenient?"

"Perfect," she said.

"Good. . . . Bishop, have we covered the main points?"

Bishop glanced down at the memo beside his coffee cup. "Everything but the most important. The tailor shop."

Carstairs nodded and brought out the piece of paper Shipkov had given him. "Here it is—the original. I suggest you make a copy now."

Mrs. Pollifax looked at the wrinkled piece of paper that had been given to Shipkov on the streets of Sofia. She read:

> *Durov, Tailor. Number 9 Vasil Levski Street*
> *Brown sheepskin vest*
> *Measurements: 40 long, 30 across back. No buttons.*
> *Give name and hotel.*
> *Tsanko will contact you.*

At the very bottom of the sheet, almost indecipherable, she read the words, *We beg help.* It was strangely poignant, this message scrawled in pencil on the soiled scrap of paper, and something of its urgency reached her as she sat in her comfortable living room thousands of miles away.

"How many passports can you send them?"

"We're going to manage eight if we can. That will take time, too, since they can't all be American. They'll probably have to be forged. Exquisitely, of course," he added with a smile.

She nodded. "Is the name Tsanko a first or a last name in Bulgaria?"

"First, I think, isn't it, Bishop?"

Bishop nodded.

"There is also . . ." Carstairs hesitated. "There is *always* the possibility that the message isn't authentic, Mrs. Pollifax. I want you to remember that. If you meet with unforeseen circumstances, you're to make a fast exit. Very fast."

"All right." She was copying the message on paper, and without glancing up she said, "I go to this shop and order a vest and then wait to be contacted. When I've given this man Tsanko the passports do I ask for anything from him?"

Carstairs frowned. "There's no bargain involved here, and he'd have every right to be affronted if we insist on anything in return. But if the occasion arises—I leave this entirely up to you—we certainly wouldn't mind learning more about a man named General Ignatov. What's his complete name, Bishop?"

"General Dimiter Kosta Ignatov," said Bishop promptly.

"You understand this Tsanko will probably know nothing. The press is state-controlled over there and the people aren't informed about much of anything," Carstairs explained. "But we'd appreciate your asking."

"I'll be glad to." Mrs. Pollifax completed her notes and handed Shipkov's message back to Carstairs, who stood up. "But you're leaving without finishing your coffee!" she told him.

"We have to. There'll be a helicopter waiting for us

at your airport in"—he glanced at his watch—"ten minutes. But I must admit it's been a real experience meeting you in your natural habitat," he said with a grin. "As well as seeing your night-blooming cereus."

"Both the night-blooming cereus and I seem to bloom once a year," she said, smiling and rising, too. "Mr. Carstairs, I shall do my very best in Bulgaria, I really will. You can count on me."

Bishop saw Carstairs open his mouth to speak, wince and close it with a snap. "Yes," he said, and then, "We'll be in touch."

"What were you about to say?" asked Bishop curiously as they descended in the elevator to the street.

Carstairs said testily, "It wasn't anything I was going to say, damn it. I just experienced the most incredibly clear memory—it came over me in waves—of how I worry about that woman when she's away."

Bishop nodded. "Yes, I believe I pointed that out to you only a few—"

"If there's one thing I can't stand it's an 'I told you so' attitude," snapped Carstairs.

"Yes, sir," Bishop said, grinning.

3

Mrs. Pollifax's preparations moved along smoothly. The next day she announced to friends and family that she would be flying to Europe soon for a visit to Yugoslavia and Bulgaria. Her daughter in Arizona was appalled. "Mother! Your first trip abroad and you're not going to visit Paris or London? You *must* visit Paris and London!" Jane tended to be somewhat managing, and Mrs. Pollifax braced herself for a long conversation.

Before telephoning her son, Roger, in Chicago, Mrs. Pollifax also braced herself, but for a different reason: Roger was a very intuitive young man.

"Bulgaria," he said now with interest. "You pick the most surprising places, Mother. Not Switzerland, France, Scotland or Belgium?"

"Bulgaria," she said firmly.

"We had the most interesting note from your neighbor Miss Hartshorne at Christmastime," he told her. "She seemed to think that you'd been here with us for a week last summer, and that Martha had been quite ill."

It was not the *non sequitur* that it sounded; Mrs.

Pollifax understood him at once. "How very odd of her to think that," she said weakly.

"Wasn't it?" He chuckled. "Whatever you're up to, Mother, I hope it's fun." And with that he blithely hung up.

The gentleman named Osmonde arrived on Thursday at ten o'clock, and was thoroughly enjoyable. Mrs. Pollifax fed him tea and macaroons and was struck by his conscientiousness: he insisted first upon seeing, measuring and photographing the coat she would wear with the hat. "For the blending, the amalgamation," he said vaguely, and she obediently buttoned herself into the quilted brown travel coat that she intended to wear on the trip.

About the hat she was as doubtful as he. Every design that he sketched looked top-heavy and he agreed this would be a problem. "You'll be carrying almost fifteen ounces in the hat," he pointed out. "Distributed, of course. Pillbox? Derby?" He sighed. "It offends the aesthetics."

"What will you do?"

"The hat itself must be very light in weight, yet look heavy enough–complicated enough–to explain its odd bulk. Perhaps a wire structure with two-inch roses covering it?"

Mrs. Pollifax winced.

"A polyethylene motor helmet?" he suggested, pencil flying, and then after a glance at Mrs. Pollifax–her cheerful round face, bright eyes and unsubdued fly-away white hair–he sighed and discreetly put that idea aside. "Will you trust me?"

"I don't want to," Mrs. Pollifax told him frankly, "but I'm due at the Art Association lunch in half an hour. I shall have to trust you."

He left with relief, carrying measurements and notes.

On the following day there were fresh instructions from Carstairs–really Mrs. Pollifax had not felt so popular since she'd won a first prize for her geraniums.

"We've come up with something to help blunt Balkan-tourist's interest in you," he said. "At least we think it may if you can wangle it. There's a chap in Sofia you might try to hire as private guide on your arrival."

Mrs. Pollifax frowned. "I don't understand. Won't Balkantourist object to my doing this?"

Carstairs' voice was dry. "They'll probably find it amusing. This man has worked for them on a number of occasions, but he drinks too much to be reliable. Our newsmen often use him when they pass through Sofia. His name is Carleton Bemish."

"Bemish," repeated Mrs. Pollifax, writing it down.

"He's an Englishman—an expatriate—who's lived in Sofia for years and speaks the language fluently. He's even married to a Bulgarian. Technically he's a free-lance correspondent—does pieces for the London papers when there's a Balkan crisis—but actually he's one of those alcoholic hangers-on who can never go home again because of some tawdry scandal or another."

"He doesn't sound very appetizing," commented Mrs. Pollifax.

"Of course not. From what I'm told he'd sell his own mother, but he'll be a helluva lot easier to lose than Balkantourist when the time comes for you to make contact. By the way, we've decided you should rent a car for your stay in Sofia. That might entice Bemish, too—he doesn't have one. Is your license up to date?"

"Yes."

"Good. Try to get Bemish," he said, and rang off.

Mrs. Pollifax added his name to her list and continued her research on Bulgaria, impressed and surprised to learn that it had been free of Turkey's oppressive rule for only some eighty years. It was the Russians who had helped liberate Bulgaria from Turkey, and it was the Russians who had liberated them later from the Nazis. It suggested a much more congenial relationship than she'd expected, and a difference from other satellite countries that intrigued her.

There was one visitor to Mrs. Pollifax's apartment, however, that she had not expected. She came home one afternoon to find her door ajar and the lock so jammed that she could not turn the key in it. Yet so far as Mrs. Pollifax could discover nothing at all had been taken. "But just see the lock," she told the policeman when he arrived.

"You're sure nothing was stolen?" he said skeptically.

"I looked very carefully while I waited for you," she told him. "The only jewelry of any value is still in the box on my bureau. I have about thirty dollars in bills and small change lying here on the bookcase—in plain sight—in the Mexican pottery bowl. Even my television set's untouched, and it's portable."

"Odd," said the policeman, looking as baffled as Mrs. Pollifax felt. "Let's make a few inquiries. Maybe someone noticed a stranger on the premises. Your burglar may have been frightened away before he got inside."

The only person who had seen anyone at all in the hall that day was Miss Hartshorne, whose apartment lay across the hall. "Yes, I saw a stranger," she said. "I'd been downtown, and was having a little trouble finding the key in my purse. So I took longer than usual, and the elevator door opened and . . ."

Mrs. Pollifax was listening, as well as the policeman, and she smiled reassuringly at her friend. "But who was it?" she asked.

"Oh, he couldn't have been your burglar," Miss Hartshorne said flatly. "He had such a good face. Cheerful. He was whistling as he came out of the elevator."

Mrs. Pollifax said firmly, "Grace, some of the most fiendish murderers have kind, cheerful faces. What man?"

"The young man who was delivering your cleaning. He held it up rather high as he came down the hall. It was on a hanger wrapped in that transparent plastic, you know. He said 'Good afternoon,' and I said 'Good afternoon' and then I found my key, unlocked my door and went in. He walked on to your door."

"What on earth made you think he went to *my* door?" asked Mrs. Pollifax. "Did you actually see him?"

Miss Hartshorne looked reproachful. "No, but I knew he was going there because he was carrying your coat, Emily. That quilted brown raincoat you wear. The new one. I could see it very clearly through the plastic."

Mrs. Pollifax looked at her thoughtfully, and then at the policeman, who had written all this down, and who now thanked Miss Hartshorne for her help. She did not say anything. She went back alone into her apartment to wait for the locksmith, but she remained thoughtful for a long time because she had not sent her quilted brown coat to the cleaner. She opened the closet door and looked inside. The coat hung there without any transparent wrappings. She took it out and examined it, then put her hand into each pocket. From one she drew out a wrinkled handkerchief with the initials EP, and from the other a bus token. She carried the coat to the window and studied it more carefully in the sunlight, but nothing appeared to be different. She put it on and observed it in the mirror. For a moment she thought it might be a shade longer than she remembered it, and then she chided herself for imagining things. She returned it to the closet.

But still it remained something of a mystery, not totally to be dismissed and apparently not to be solved until Miss Hartshorne changed her mind about its being this particular coat she'd seen.

A week later Mrs. Pollifax left for the Balkans wearing the coat and her new custom-made hat. She had misjudged Osmonde. He had produced a marvelously imaginative hat, and just the kind that she enjoyed most. It was an inflated, cushiony bird's nest made out of soft woven straw with a small feathered bird perched at the peak. It was true that it had a tendency to tilt, but Mrs. Pollifax skewered it sternly in place with three stout hatpins.

"You *what?*" said Bishop incredulously. He had been on vacation for a week—his first vacation in five years —and he had returned only the day before. Now a cable had arrived from Bulgaria that was utterly mystifying to Bishop. It lay on the desk between them in Carstairs' office. It read:

COAT FOR 10573 CLEARED OKAY AND IN POSSESSION, WILL PROCEED AS DIRECTED.

10573 was Mrs. Pollifax's file number.

Carstairs sighed. "I told you, it's this damn economy drive. Upstairs insisted. Budgetwise, it took two experienced men a week to forge those passports, and then there were Mrs. Pollifax's travel expenses, not to mention Osmonde's bill for the hat. As they pointed out Upstairs, we get nothing but good will out of sending eight forged passports into Bulgaria. It's not enough to justify the expense. I was told this *flatly*. I had to share my courier."

Bishop said accusingly, "This cable is from Assen Radev."

"Yes, by way of Belgrade, Frankfurt, London and Baltimore. It came out with his weekly delivery of *pâté de foie gras.*"

Bishop's coldness turned glacial. "Radev's one of our nasties—you know that—and you've always sworn you'd keep Mrs. Pollifax out of the heavy stuff."

"I told you this was *not* my idea," Carstairs reminded him irritably. "They had to get some things to Radev, I had already engaged Mrs. Pollifax and briefed her for a simple courier job. What could I do? Radev has been sent Mrs. Pollifax's original coat. A duplicate coat was made—an exact copy, but fitted with the papers—and smuggled into Mrs. Pollifax's apartment. They're doubling up assignments everywhere."

"Then perhaps you can explain why the hell you didn't tell Mrs. Pollifax she's going into Bulgaria loaded for bear!"

Carstairs sighed. "Because she only goes through Customs 'loaded for bear,' as you call it, and as soon as she's entered Bulgaria, Radev will quietly exchange coats with her. She won't even know about it. I decided that was wisest. She's only an amateur, you know."

"I'm surprised you remember that," Bishop said bitterly. "I think it's shocking you didn't tell her. I suppose you've considered the possibility that Radev could have a heart attack before he can switch coats—or get clipped by a car?"

Carstairs said evenly, "Traffic is extremely light in Sofia, and I understand the rate of cardiac seizure in Bulgaria is very low. Something to do with all that yogurt they eat." He shook his head. "I'm afraid you're losing your usual sense of detachment, Bishop."

"Detachment! I don't even dare ask what's hidden in that coat—"

"It's better you not," Carstairs assured him gravely. "This isn't Sears Roebuck or Gimbels, you know. We're heels in the CIA, Bishop—outcasts and sinners and heels. Try to remember that."

Bishop's lips thinned. "Outcasts, yes. Sinners possibly. Heels obviously. But I thought we were at least *gentlemen*," he said coldly, and walked out, closing the door sharply behind him.

4

Mrs. Pollifax sat in the Belgrade air terminal and waited patiently for TABSO to announce its flight to Sofia. She was quite ready for departure. The wild gray cliffs of Yugoslavia, its friendly people, the incredible blue of the Adriatic had relaxed and charmed her, but now there was work to do.

She had arrived early because she enjoyed watching departures. The planes for Frankfurt, Budapest, Dubrovnik and Brussels had been announced and had presumably left. Now she guessed all the remaining travelers were bound for Sofia, and her glance returned to a group of young people who occupied the corner of the lounge. She had been covertly observing them for some time, certain that two of them were Americans. She had expected them to leave on the plane for Brussels, but they were still here. They were bare-legged, tanned and long-haired—boys and girls alike—and instead of luggage they carried dusty packs on their backs.

They looked as though they were quarreling now, and as she watched, one of the girls lifted her voice and said furiously, "But I told you! All of us don't want to go to Bulgaria, can't you understand?"

"Debby, you're shouting."

"Why shouldn't I shout? I feel like shouting!"

Mrs. Pollifax frankly eavesdropped.

"Phil, for instance—and me, too," the American girl said. "And last night Andre admitted he wasn't all that interested either."

Her anger appeared to be directed at the stocky dark young man who seemed to be in charge of the group. He looked less a student than the others, older and harder. Now he gesticulated in reply. "We have the visas, yes? You think it easy to get visas to Bulgaria? Why the hell not?" His was an accent Mrs. Pollifax found difficult to pinpoint—Yugoslavian, perhaps. In any case he sounded insulted by this revolt, and very angry indeed.

"But none of us really thought they'd give us visas!" flung out the American girl. "And Phil's got dysentery, and I just think it's—"

"We voted, didn't we?"

"Nikki and Debby, stop arguing," said the French girl flatly, and they all looked at her, and the ginger-haired English boy threw her a kiss and the third girl laughed and said something in German that caused them all to laugh.

All except the American boy named Phil, who picked up his knapsack and carried it to the bench beside Mrs. Pollifax and sat down.

"Trouble?" asked Mrs. Pollifax cheerfully.

He turned and stared at her and she in turn looked at him. He seemed a very *nice* young man. Disreputable, of course, in those filthy jeans and all that untidy black hair, but his eyes were a marvelous shade of intense blue and the height of his cheekbones gave his face an interesting shape.

The boy nodded; she had been approved. "We're getting damn sick of each other," he said bluntly.

Mrs. Pollifax smiled. "It happens. Have you been together long?"

He shrugged. "Some of us. But we were doing fine until Nikki came along. I'm beginning to hate his guts."

"That would be the bossy, dark young man?"

"Yeah, that's Nikki," he said, and they both stared across at Nikki, whose back was turned to them. "He showed up in Dubrovnik two weeks ago. Debby I met in Vienna—she's great—and she'd already met Ghislaine in Paris. Erika and Andre joined us on the road later, but Nikki—"

"Obviously the executive type," said Mrs. Pollifax sympathetically. Noting the expression on the young man's face she added sharply, "Are you all right?"

"Damn dysentery," he said. His face had gone white and he leaned over in pain, guarding himself by hugging his stomach with his arms.

"But haven't you medicine for it?"

He shook his head. "I lost it yesterday, but Nikki's feeding me his." He lifted his head and said with a little laugh, "Maybe I'll have to go along to Bulgaria with him just to stay with his pills. Actually I'm here only to see them off. I don't want to go to Bulgaria. No—I can't make up my mind." He laughed savagely. "Mind! I don't have any mind, it's gone all groggy."

Mrs. Pollifax said in alarm, "You poor boy, you look terribly pale and your speech is slurred. I think you're really ill."

"Dubrovnik," he said dreamily. "That's where we were and that's where I'd like to be."

"I've just come from there," Mrs. Pollifax told him, nodding. "It's magnificent, isn't it? I was there for the Music Festival."

He turned and looked at her. "You, too? Man, that was something, wasn't it? Those rock walls, the sea, the sky like velvet—" He abruptly yawned. "Damn it, now I'm sleepy—one extreme or the other, dysentery or stupor."

"The right medicine would cure both," she told him sternly.

He shook his head as if to clear it. "I'll get some. Do you have any idea what this says?" He pulled a piece of paper from his pocket and handed it to her. "I can't even tell what language it is."

Mrs. Pollifax glanced down at the wrinkled, narrow slip of paper on which several sentences had been printed, followed by a series of numbers. "That's the Cyrillic alphabet, isn't it?" she said, frowning over it. "It looks rather like a pass to a swimming pool, or a lottery ticket. Where did you get it?"

Phil laughed. "I picked somebody's pocket."

At that moment the loudspeaker system crackled with life and began to announce the departure of the TABSO flight for Sofia in four different languages, the voices echoing and re-echoing through the terminal. Further conversation became impossible and Mrs. Pollifax held out her hand to the young man. "Emily Pollifax," she shouted at him over the din. "Delighted to have met you. And please—do see a doctor about your dysentery."

He arose, too, blushed slightly and extended a hand in the manner of one remembering a nearly forgotten ritual. "Philip Trenda," he shouted as they shook hands. Abruptly a new system of pain crossed his face and he doubled up.

The American girl with the waist-length hair—they had called her Debby—was suddenly at his side. "Phil, this is awful—you're really sick."

"I'll walk to the plane with you," he said.

"That's stupid. You ought to sit or lie down, not *walk*."

His mouth tightened. "I'm not sick and I'm going to walk you to the plane."

"Your piece of paper," called Mrs. Pollifax.

He vaguely gestured it aside as he shouldered his pack and joined the girl. Mrs. Pollifax dropped the slip of paper into her purse, picked up her flight bag and followed the group of young people toward the gate. There she saw them re-group—yes, and resume their quarreling.

With a shake of her head Mrs. Pollifax gave up her ticket, received her seat number and boarded the plane. The young people arrived several minutes later and noisily made their way to the plane's rear. The young man name Philip was with them.

She thought, He shouldn't have let them talk him into coming. Not with dysentery. But that was the way travel was: a series of chance encounters, fleeting involvements, motives never explained, endings never known. Firmly she put aside all thought of the young American and fastened her seat belt. As they taxied down the runway for takeoff she opened a tattered copy of *Newsweek*.

But as the plane lifted, Mrs. Pollifax realized that printed words were lifeless to her at a moment when she was about to begin another courier assignment. She put down the magazine and gazed out of the window, wondering what she would be like when she finished this job because it seemed to her that each one left her changed. Now, once again, she was leaving behind friends, identity, children, possessions—everything secure —for another small adventure. At her age, too. But this was exactly the age, she thought, when life ought to be spent, not hoarded. There had been enough years of comfortable living, and complacency was nothing but delusion. One could not always change the world, she felt, but one could change oneself.

The plane had begun to decelerate. Glancing at her watch Mrs. Pollifax saw that it was much too early for them to be reaching Sofia. A voice began an announcement over the loudspeaker in Bulgarian, then in French, in German and at last in English: they were making an unscheduled stop in Rumania. The delay would be brief. No one was to leave the plane.

They landed. From her window Mrs. Pollifax could see a sign at some distance that said TRIASCA REPUBLIC

SOCIALIST RUMANIA in huge red letters. Down the aisle an Englishman grumbled to his companion. "They never explain things in these countries. Or apologize."

"Police state, of course. I always wonder if they're going to arrest someone aboard or search our luggage. I say, it looks as if this stop's for someone special."

"Some high mucky-muck, eh?"

"Looks it."

"Isn't that General Ignatov? You were in Sofia last year. Bloody tiresome the way his picture was in the party newspaper week after week."

General Ignatov? Mrs. Pollifax turned to her window and saw a number of people making their way across the field to the plane. There was a comic-opera look about the procession. It was led by a tall, darkly handsome man wearing a uniform that fairly dripped medals. He was walking with long strides and cutting the air with a walking stick. Behind him two army officers had to break into a trot to keep up with him. Following them came a swarm of men in business suits.

Under Mrs. Pollifax's window the general halted, the others surrounded him and everyone shook hands. As the general moved slightly apart she saw him clearly. What a powerful face, she thought in surprise. He was laughing now, his teeth very white against his dark skin, his head thrown back in a posture of amusement, but she did not believed he was amused. She had the impression that he had taught himself to laugh because otherwise he would be all arrogance, cruelty, tension and energy.

A moment later he boarded the plane and she glimpsed him again as he paused in the space between tourist and first-class. He was issuing sharp orders now to the stewardess; the charm had vanished and he looked only brutal.

Mrs. Pollifax shivered. There was nothing comic-opera about this general. She suddenly understood that she was entering an iron curtain country, and that she was going to contact there a group that was defying all the power this man represented. She realized that General Ignatov could squash that group under the heel of one boot. He would squash her, too, if she crossed his line of vision. And under the bird in her hat she carried eight very illicit passports.

5

No one was allowed to leave the plane in Sofia until General Ignatov and his two officers had disembarked. Mrs. Pollifax spent these minutes in anchoring her hat more securely and in trying to forget that she carried contraband. She remembered saying to Carstairs in her apartment, "I suppose in a country like Bulgaria these passports are the equivalent of gold."

"Not gold," he'd said. "Tell me first what the equivalent of a human life is, and perhaps then we can measure their value. Perhaps."

Once passengers were allowed to leave, Mrs. Pollifax descended from the plane and followed the others into the terminal. As she approached Customs she reminded herself that she was only a tourist, and fairly experienced at dissembling. She was also—thanks to retired police chief Lorvale Brown—moderately adept at karate, but still she could not remember when she had felt so nervous. She watched her suitcase opened and a pair of hands methodically sift its contents. The Customs man then looked at her, his eyes narrowing as they came to rest

on the bird atop her hat. Mrs. Pollifax braced herself.
A look of astonishment crossed his face, he smiled,
nudged his companion and pointed to the bird. Two pairs
of eyes regarded her hat in surprise, and then the first
officer gave her an admiring grin and signaled her to
move on. Happily she obeyed. She had passed Customs.
There was only Balkantourist left to confront, and presumably in time her knees would stop trembling.

Carstairs had described Bulgarians as the realists
among the Balkan people. "Also the most trustworthy,"
he had said crisply. "They'll never knife you in the back."

"That's reassuring," Mrs. Pollifax had said.

He had added gravely, "They'll wait instead for you
to turn around first."

She was reminded of this by the Balkantourist representative who awaited her beyond Customs. The square,
compact young woman greeted her with a hearty manner, but her eyes were surprisingly indifferent, almost
contemptuous. Her face was high cheekboned and boy-
ish and devoid of makeup; she wore a wrinkled khaki
dress with insignia at each lapel. "I am Nevena," she said
in a husky voice, heavily accented, and turning her back
on Mrs. Pollifax she continued joking vivaciously with
several of the Customs men. This left Mrs. Pollifax to
cope with her luggage. She locked her suitcase, put away
her passport and, luggage in hand, waited. Apparently
Nevena was well known. Obviously she was in no hurry.

It was tiresome standing first on one foot and then
the other. Mrs. Pollifax's glance strayed from Nevena and
toward the dwindling line at Customs. Her eyes fell upon
the group of young travelers from the Belgrade air terminal and she saw that again they appeared to be having
problems, this time with Customs. Philip was propped
against the counter smothering a yawn. Debby looked
discouraged. Nikki however, was still gesturing, his face
livid as he argued with the man behind the counter. All
of this Mrs. Pollifax noted in the flash of a second, just

as a new official arrived to resolve the quarrel. He directed the group out of line and herded them to a far corner of the hall.

She interrupted Nevena firmly. "I'm going back through Customs," she announced. "I see that some friends of mine are having trouble over there, they may need help."

Nevena's frown was not encouraging. "Help?" she said gruffly.

Mrs. Pollifax pointed. "In the corner, see?"

Nevena's gaze followed her hand and then swerved back to give Mrs. Pollifax a quick, hard scrutiny. "Those peoples are known to you?"

"Yes."

Nevena shook her head. Her eyes rested again on Mrs. Pollifax, curious and a little startled. "The man speaking with thcm is not a Customs man. We go now."

"But I really think—"

"We go," Nevena said sharply, and tugged at Mrs. Pollifax's elbow, propelling her toward the door.

"I don't understand," said Mrs. Pollifax, resisting.

Nevena stopped just outside the building. "If they are in trouble you cannot help them."

"Why should they be in trouble?"

"That is a man from security questioning them. You wish to be in trouble, too?"

"Security?" echoed Mrs. Pollifax.

"The car is here," Nevena said sternly, pointing and opening the door. "Come–inside."

Mrs. Pollifax hesitated and then remembered that trouble was a luxury she couldn't afford and that security was a synonym for the secret police. With a sigh she climbed into the car. "What kind of trouble?" she persisted as Nevena joined her.

Nevena shrugged. "Maybe the visas are in disorder?"

Mrs. Pollifax relaxed. If that was the case then the group would be flown back to Yugoslavia and their squabbles over visiting Bulgaria would be ended. Nevertheless she had been reminded that it was not healthy to be singled out by the police here. She really *must* be cautious.

"Now," said Nevena as she started the car, "I speak to you of Sofia, which is some five thousand years old and is capital of Bulgaria. It is fourth Bulgarian capital after Pliska, Preslav and Tarnovo. The Thracians called it Serdika, the Slavs called it Sredets, the Byzantines, Triaditsa. Although destroyed and burned by Goths, Magyars, Huns, Patsinaks and Crusaders, Sofia is today a beautiful modern city. With its original historical and cultural monuments and numerous mineral springs our capital is a great attraction for tourists. . . ."

Oh dear, thought Mrs. Pollifax, suppressing a yawn, and in revolt she began her own assessment of Sofia, whose low silhouette lay stretched out ahead of her in the clear sparkling air. It was a sprawling city that encircled the foothill of a long high mountain range. The air was bracing and everything looked clean and fresh. Along the road grew clumps of Queen Anne's lace, oddly endearing to her after the brief chill that had visited her. She decided that she really must halt that droning, mechanical voice at her side. It was time to assert.

"There's a gentleman I would like to call on tomorrow," she told Nevena. "If you'll advise me how to find him."

Nevena's face tightened. "You *know* someone in my country?"

Mrs. Pollifax shook her head. Speaking each word slowly and clearly she explained, "I don't *know* this man. He's not even Bulgarian. His name was suggested to me by a friend, in case I wanted to learn more about your country. His name is Carleton Bemish."

"Oh—Mistair Beemish!" laughed Nevena, and her face sprang to life, gamine and suddenly pretty. "The funny one! Everyone knows Bemish." She said firmly, "He would be the good man for you if he is not busy. Maybe he have time. For myself I have not enough time, but you could join a group I begin tomorrow. At 1 P.M. sharp they tour Sofia in Balkantourist bus. Very *nice* bus."

"I'm renting a car while I'm here," pointed out Mrs. Pollifax.

"Oh–" Nevena slapped a hand to her forehead. "You are accurate! Eleven tomorrow." She slowed the car. "Mr. Bemish live there," she said, pointing to a narrow, modern cement building punctuated by very symmetrical balconies. "Only five squares from your hotel. I write the address for you in Bulgarian when you wish."

Mrs. Pollifax turned, affixing the look of the building in her mind. "Thank you," she said, and began to make a mental note of the corners they passed.

Within minutes they entered a plaza lined with modern shops and dominated by a towering granite and glass building. "Your hotel," pointed out Nevena proudly.

And despite the lettering across the front that in no way resembled Rila, it proved to be the Hotel Rila. Nevena parked at a side entrance with stairs leading into a small side lobby. "It is now 3 P.M.," she said with a stern glance at her wristwatch. "I register you at hotel and then there is time for me personally to show you Sofia. Maybe one and a half hours, very quick but–"

Very politely Mrs. Pollifax said, "Another day that would be pleasant, but I'd really prefer to rest now."

Nevena gave her a sharp glance. "You are old?"

"Very," said Mrs. Pollifax.

Nevena nodded. "You give me passport, I register you." At the desk she spoke severely in Bulgarian to the clerk and then turned to Mrs. Pollifax. "Okay, I go now. At 11 A.M. tomorrow sharp I meet you beside this desk when car arrives. The man who brings car speaks no English."

"That's very kind of you."

"This man who takes suitcase up for you, give him

only a few *stotynki,* you understand? This is not a capitalist country."

Mrs. Pollifax nodded and watched her march out of the lobby. She wondered what someone like Nevena—so stolid, so efficient—would do with the two free hours she'd just been given. Certainly not rest, she thought, but then Mrs. Pollifax had no intention of resting either. Having just won herself a few hours of unexpected privacy, she thought it an excellent time to begin her sub rosa work. She would visit Durov's tailor shop.

6

Nothing in this hotel district of Sofia was shabby. Everything was clean, bare, new, the boulevards almost empty of traffic. Map in hand, Mrs. Pollifax crossed Vasil Levski street to number nine and studied the word printed across the glass window: it said ШИВа4 This was not particularly helpful. She peered through the glass. Seeing the bolts of fabrics hanging along the walls, she walked inside to find two men and a woman bent over the hems and seams of fabric in their laps. The stolid-faced woman with gray hair left her sewing machine and walked to the counter. "Do you speak English?" asked Mrs. Pollifax.

The older man in the rear looked up suddenly. Without a word the woman returned to her machine and the man came forward. "Pliss?" he said cautiously. "I speak the English."

"I would like to take home a man's sheepskin jacket or vest," she told him.

"Ah—we have fine skins," he said, nodding.

"Good." She met his eye before adding, "I want a brown vest for a friend in America."

"A brown one!" he said with pleasure. "Not black?"

She shook her head. "Brown. Here are the measurements." She offered them on a slip of paper.

The expression on his face remained totally unchanged. He copied the measurements arduously, chewing on his underlip as he labored. He lifted his head. "You stay at a hotel?"

"The Rila," she replied, and aware that the sign on her hotel bore no resemblance to the word, she brought out the hotel's leaflet and showed him its picture.

"Yes. Your name?"

"Mrs. Pollifax."

"Pollifax." She noticed that he made no move to write down either her name or the name of her hotel. "Excuse, pliss?" he said formally, and abruptly disappeared into the back room. Over the whirring of the sewing machines she could hear him speaking, perhaps on the telephone for she heard no answering voice. A few minutes later he returned. "The vest will cost"—he pursed his lips thoughtfully—"maybe twelve *leva,* maybe eighteen."

"Wonderful," exclaimed Mrs. Pollifax, quite carried away by the thought of paying only six or nine dollars for a sheepskin vest until she remembered it was an imaginary vest they discussed.

"We let you know. Maybe tomorrow, okay?" For the first time he gave her a glance that she could read as meaningful, and she nodded.

"Thank you," she said, and left.

Mrs. Pollifax walked slowly back to her hotel, pausing to look into a number of stores to prove that her interest was not limited to tailoring shops, should anyone be following her. When she reached the hotel and her room on the sixth floor, she discovered that she felt a great deal lighter: a grave responsibility had been lifted from her, she had found the shop and notified the Underground of her arrival. The rest would be up to the man named Tsanko now, and in the meantime she could relax and begin to enjoy Sofia.

After unpacking the top inch of her suitcase, she took a quick shower and then dressed. She felt quite stimulated by the brief exchange of words at number nine Vasil Levski. The man had reminded her of Mr. Omelianuk, the owner of the little delicatessen around the corner from her apartment in New Brunswick, and she reflected how alike people were, no matter where they lived. The problems changed, but people were the same. She wondered how she would be contacted, and when. Apparently not this evening; the man had implied tomorrow. That was disappointing, especially when she glanced at her watch and saw that it was only six o'clock. It seemed much too early for dinner, and in any case she wasn't hungry.

I'm feeling too efficient to be hungry, she thought, and it suddenly occurred to her that she might complete all of tomorrow's work today by calling upon Mr. Carleton Bemish. Perhaps she could persuade him to join her for dinner. Failing that, she could at least engage him for a sightseeing tour of Sofia tomorrow in her rented car.

Splendid idea, she decided, and putting on her hat she descended in the elevator to the small side lobby and walked outside to begin her search for Mr. Bemish's street and apartment house. One left turn, she remembered, and then four blocks to the Rila, which meant—turning it backward—that she walked four blocks away from the plaza and turned to the right. And there it was, giving her cause to congratulate herself on accomplishing so much during her first hours in Bulgaria.

But what a bleak-looking place the building was on closer scrutiny. It looked new, and very clean, but it had been constructed in the stark, concrete-modern style of the twenties that aimed at simplicity but succeeded only in looking utilitarian. Mrs. Pollifax entered a lobby that resembled a laundry room, with a drain placed squarely in the center of the floor; there were two couches, of tubular steel and hard plastic, at right angles along the wall. A directory of occupants gave Bemish's name, apartment 301, in both Bulgarian and English. A windowless staircase, also cement, led up to an unseen landing from which drifted the smell of cabbage. There was no elevator.

Mrs. Pollifax began to climb, and as she climbed the smell of cabbage grew stronger and the ill-placed ceiling lights grew more garish. At the door of apartment 301 she knocked and waited. The building was quiet, but from inside 301 came the sound of someone singing. It was a man's voice, overcharged, belligerent and rendered in a spirit that Mrs. Pollifax guessed did not come from any internal source of well-being. Mr. Bemish's cocktail hour had begun some hours ago.

The door opened and a cheerful, rotund man beamed at her.

"Mr. Bemish?" she said. "Mr. Carleton Bemish?"

He winked. "In the flesh."

And indeed her first impression was of flesh, rather a lot of it, and all of it arranged in circles: a plump round stomach, round face, round chins, small round eyes embedded in circles of flesh, and a small round mouth. He gave the impression of vast jovialness until Mrs. Pollifax looked directly into his eyes and found them curiously empty, like stones.

"I'm Mrs. Pollifax," she said. "May I come in? I was told that . . ." She paused doubtfully. He stood blocking her entrance; she stopped and waited.

"Something nice, I hope?" he asked with a second wink.

"Told that I might talk with you," she said, and firmly walked past him into his living room. It was very bold of her, but she had already gained the impression that Mr. Bemish was not in full command of his faculties. "About a job," she said. "As my guide for several days."

Off to the right a door closed, but not before she had caught a glimpse of a drab, mouse-like little woman fleeing the room; a cleaning woman, perhaps, although the apartment did not look as if it had been cleaned in years.

"I couldn't be less interested," said Carleton Bemish, following her into the room. "I'm otherwise occupied. Busy. Very busy."

And very prosperous, too, noticed Mrs. Pollifax as her glance fell on a heavily draped round table in the center of the room. On it stood a silver bucket with a bottle of champagne protruding from it. It was a startling sight in such a shabby room. She said mechanically, "I'm sorry, you're expecting someone?"

"My dear woman, of course I'm expecting someone," he said pompously, rocking a little on his heels. "A man like myself has many important friends. Many."

Her glance fell to the couch near the table and she saw long white cardboard boxes piled there. From one of them spilled the shimmering folds of a brocade dressing gown. His glance followed hers and he beamed. "Not bad, hmm?" he said, walking over to the couch. He pulled the robe from the box and held it up. "They're not under-estimating Carleton Bemish any more! Look at it—pure silk!"

"Ah, you've inherited money," suggested Mrs. Pollifax.

He draped the robe across his shoulders and winked at her. "What I've inherited is a news story—the biggest —and I've made the news story myself. I feel surprisingly like God!" He came near to Mrs. Pollifax, the robe streaming behind him like a train, his breath suffocatingly alcoholic. With intense scorn, and breathing heavily at her, he said, "They're no longer saying 'Good old Bemish, nice old Bemish'. . . . They treat me with respect now, I can tell you." He tapped his right temple meaningfully. "Brains. Wit. That's what it takes to survive, Mrs.—what's your name?"

"Pollifax."

"The thing is," he said defiantly, "I'm not up for hire. Carleton Bemish is no longer a has-been. You understand?"

Mrs. Pollifax sighed. "I understand. You're no longer a has-been."

He peered suspiciously into her face. "That sounds damn impertinent."

"You're standing on my right foot," said Mrs. Pollifax frankly.

He jumped back. "Oh–sorry."

She nodded. "I quite understand now that you're not available, and so I'll just run along. In the meantime I'll be looking forward to reading your news story."

He beamed appreciatively. *"With* by-line. Already posted–to London, Paris, New York. But not," he added owlishly, "in Sofia. Not in this country. Pity about that."

Thoroughly tired of this, Mrs. Pollifax moved to the door; he was suddenly there before her, his mood changed again. "Wait a minute," he said suspiciously. "Who did you say you are?"

"Mrs. Pollifax," she sighed. "I came to see you about guiding–"

He relaxed. "Oh yes, I remember."

Someone else had arrived at Mr. Bemish's door and was knocking. "My guest!" said Carleton Bemish happily, and threw open the door, exclaiming in Bulgarian to the man who stood there illuminated by the overhead hall light. His face was clearly outlined and Mrs. Pollifax stared at him in surprise. She knew him. He in turn glanced at her with barely concealed impatience and addressed himself to Bemish, the two of them speaking in rapid Bulgarian.

She knew him, but from where? He was young, very dark, square and broad-shouldered. "The Belgrade air terminal!" she said aloud.

The young man turned and looked at her. "I beg your pardon?"

"You're Nikki," she said in surprise. "You were in Philip's group. What was his name, Philip Trenda?"

Carleton Bemish's mouth dropped open. He turned to look incredulously at Nikki.

"Oh?" said Nikki, heavy brows lifting. "You were there, perhaps?" he added smoothly.

"Yes indeed," she told him warmly. "And later I saw your group led away from the Customs line by the police, and I wanted to come over and . . ." She stopped. The atmosphere almost crackled with shocks. Carleton Bemish's eyes were growing larger and rounder while Nikki's eyes were growing narrower. She added limply, "But you're—all right? They didn't bother you?"

Nikki bowed stiffly. "A small misunderstanding, no more." He looked at her curiously. "You say that you knew Philip?"

"I didn't say so," she pointed out. "We had a brief but very interesting chat in the air terminal, that's all. Now I really must leave," she said. "Please remember me to Philip when you see him," she told Nikki, and over her shoulder to them both, "Good night."

Neither man responded. She had the feeling that she left them dazed, but she couldn't honestly attribute it to the force of her personality. She wondered what she'd said that so took them by surprise.

The smell of cabbage was stronger in the hall, reminding Mrs. Pollifax of her own hunger and of the increasing lateness of the hour. She hurried back to her hotel.

Mrs. Pollifax dined alone with a small sense of letdown that aborted her appetite. First of all the food in the hotel restaurant was imitation American, the peas straight from a can, and yet—perversely—no one, not even the headwaiter, knew the English language; a contact with Tsanko appeared impossible for another twelve or fifteen hours, and Carleton Bemish was not available at all. She told herself that she was experiencing the effects of her first hours in a strange country far from home, although this was of small consolation to her frame of mind, which was gloomy.

It was not until she was in the middle of dessert that it suddenly struck her how very odd it was that Bemish's guest had turned out to be Nikki. How did it happen that a hitchhiking Yugoslavian student was on such friendly terms with a man who lived in Sofia?

I know many, many important people, Bemish had said defiantly.

The thought so startled her that she looked up in astonishment to meet the eye of a small gray-haired man in a gray suit who was watching her closely from a table near the entrance. He glanced away so swiftly that she gave him a second look, at once curious and alerted. He was short and stolid, his suit badly cut and his whole appearance so remarkably anonymous that she would never have noticed him except for his stare. She had the impression that he had only recently arrived, and this was confirmed by a glance at his table, still empty of food.

Perhaps it was Tsanko, she thought hopefully, and perhaps contact would be made soon, after all.

She paid her bill and went upstairs, but no one knocked on her door and no messages were slipped under the rug. Rather sadly, she retired at half-past ten.

7

Sometime during the night Mrs. Pollifax experienced a nightmare in which she was lying helplessly in bed at home and being observed by a burglar who had entered her room. She was not accustomed to nightmares and as she fought her way back to consciousness she discovered that she was indeed in bed, it was night and a man was standing at the foot of the bed looking down at her. He was clearly silhouetted against the window.

Mrs. Pollifax waited, breath suspended, for the man to identify himself as Tsanko. He did not. He moved stealthily away from the foot of the bed and went toward the closet, where he turned on a small flashlight. He leaned over the lock, his back to her.

If he wasn't Tsanko, she thought indignantly, then he must be a plain, old-fashioned burglar, and without stopping to consider the risks Mrs. Pollifax slid out of her bed and stood up. Carefully tiptoeing along the wall she came up behind the man, flattened her right hand and delivered a medium karate chop to the side of his neck—at least she hoped it was only a medium blow—and watched him sink to the floor.

Switching on the lights she saw there was no doubt at all that the man was a thief because he held her brown quilted coat in his arms. He lay on his side, half of the coat trapped under him, a relatively young man wearing a black suit and black tie. Stepping over him she went to the telephone and picked up the receiver. "I have a burglar in my room," she told the desk clerk coldly.

The reply was depressing and sounded like, *"Murdekoochinko lesso razenum."*

"Burglar. Thief!" she said. "Does anyone speak English?"

"Anglichanin? Ameryerikanski?"

Mrs. Pollifax grimly put down the phone, stepped again over the man and opened the door. She peered outside; the halls were deserted. Leaving her door open she walked down to the elevator, but there was no one there either. With a sigh she stepped into it and descended to the lobby.

There were two men at the desk, and it was a full two minutes before they were able to control their surprise at seeing Mrs. Pollifax emerge from the elevator in flowered pajamas. It was at least another several minutes before they understood that she wanted them to return to her room with her, and this appeared to induce in them an even deeper state of shock. Neither of them spoke English and it was necessary for them to identify her by their desk records. When this had been done they telephoned Balkantourist.

A peevish Nevena was reached at last. "It is 3 A.M.," she announced furiously.

"I have a burglar lying on the floor of my hotel room," Mrs. Pollifax told her.

This was translated by Nevena to the room clerk, who stared at Mrs. Pollifax incredulously.

The phone was handed back to Mrs. Pollifax. "We do

not have thieves in Bulgaria," Nevena said coldly, and then with outrageous illogic, "You should not encourage such matters by not locking your closet and your door."

"I locked both the doors to the closet and the door to my room," said Mrs. Pollifax crisply. "I placed the key to the closet under my pillow and slept on it. But the man had already broken into the closet because he had my brown quilted coat in his arms. I saw it."

Orders were given to the hotel clerks, one of whom gestured Mrs. Pollifax to the elevator and returned with her to the sixth floor. He accompanied her to her room, where the door remained open. He first looked inside, cautiously.

Mrs. Pollifax followed him in. The room was empty. "He's gone," she said indignantly. "He's gotten away."

The desk clerk pointed to the door of the closet and looked at her questioningly. For a moment Mrs. Pollifax didn't understand, and then she saw that the door was locked. She went to her pillow. The key had not been touched, and removing it she returned to the closet. With the desk clerk watching she unlocked and opened the door.

Her coat was hanging in the closet, as well as her clothes. The hat was on the shelf. Nothing had been touched.

In open-mouthed astonishment—for she had just seen her coat *out* of the closet—she turned to the desk clerk. It needed only one glance to understand what he thought. "Amerikanski," he muttered indignantly, and left.

What Nevena's reaction would be to the locked closet taxed Mrs. Pollifax's imagination. This time before retiring, however, she placed two chairs in front of her door and hid the key to the closet under the mattress.

On first encounter Nevena gave no indication of her anger during the night. She was delighted to find Mrs.

Pollifax waiting. "You still wish to advance by yourself, on the wheels?"

"Yes indeed, and I've decided to drive to the TV tower on Mount Vitosha. It'll be easiest to find because I can see it ahead of me while I drive."

"Good! You may also wish to try the cable car—it goes down, then up—splendid views! For lunch the Kopitoto is good, very good. Here is the driver." She waved to him vigorously and ushered Mrs. Pollifax outside to the door of a trim little green Volkswagen. "You are certain?" she demanded.

Mrs. Pollifax looked at the car and felt a wave of doubt. Then, "I'm certain," she said and climbed in, turned the key in the ignition and heard the purring of the engine.

But Nevena insisted upon having the last word. She leaned over the window, her eyes suddenly brimming with glee. "Be certain nobody steals the pretty brown coat again, eh, Mrs. Pollifax?" she shouted into her ear.

8

An hour later Mrs. Pollifax was seated triumphantly on the terrace of the Kopitoto restaurant, a mountain breeze ruffling the bird on her hat and Sofia lying at her feet. Marvelous, she thought, gazing around her appreciatively, and as her glance roamed the terrace with its bright little tables she saw that either Sofia was a very small town indeed, or she was beginning to know a surprising number of people. She saw first of all the small gray man from the hotel dining room the evening before. He was just seating himself, and she thought his arrival four minutes after her own was an interesting development. It was of course a very scenic place in which to lunch; it was also possible that he was a fellow tourist, perhaps visiting Sofia from another Balkan country, but she was not inclined to think so: he looked so particularly joyless.

The second person she recognized on the terrace was the American girl Debby, from the group at the Belgrade air terminal. Although Philip was missing, it was otherwise the same group of young people. One of them arose

–it was Nikki, still talking aggressively, with gestures. He was abruptly cut off from view by the arrival of her waiter.

Mrs. Pollifax ordered and ate her lunch. Finished, she gathered up coat and purse and looked across the terrace. Phil had still not rejoined the group and Nikki was just leaving, smiling and formally shaking hands with each member of the party. Mrs. Pollifax watched him go and then crossed the terrace.

"Good afternoon," she said cheerfully. "We traveled together here on the same plane from Belgrade. Are you enjoying Sofia?"

Five faces turned blankly to her.

"It was Phil I spoke with," she explained, dropping into the chair Nikki had vacated. "Is he with you today?"

The American girl promptly burst into tears.

"Mon cheri," said the pale young man softly, grasping her wrist.

"Is she ill?" asked Mrs. Pollifax anxiously.

"It's Phil," explained the other girl. "You mentioned Phil."

"Yes, I was concerned about his dysentery. How is he? Or rather, where is he?"

"In prison—here in Sofia," blurted out Debby with a sob. "They've arrested him."

"Arrested him!" cried Mrs. Pollifax.

The ginger-haired British boy nodded. "The idiots seem to think he's some kind of spy."

"Phil a spy," Debby repeated angrily. She drew a sodden handkerchief from her pocket and wiped her eyes. "I remember you," she said abruptly. "You did talk to Phil and now he's—and in Bulgaria of all places!" She burst into tears again.

"But I don't understand," protested Mrs. Pollifax. "What on earth happened?"

The young Frenchman turned to her and in precise

English and a soft voice explained. "First they questioned us at Customs—"

"Who did?" asked Mrs. Pollifax, wondering if they shared Nevena's knowledge of uniforms.

He shrugged. "The uniforms were different. We do not know since we don't speak their language. Nikki was upset—"

"In what language was he upset?" asked Mrs. Pollifax quickly.

Again he shrugged. "Who knows? He is—Yugoslavian, isn't he?" he asked the others. "In any case he was very angry—in what language I don't know," he added with a soft smile for Mrs. Pollifax, "and they took him away, into another room. A few minutes later he came and said okay, it was a small misunderstanding."

She nodded; that sounded familiar.

"Then we decided to be stoppers—"

"That's what they call hitchhikers here," put in the girl.

"Except no one picked us up so we kept walking, stopping only once—"

"To take a picture—"

"Phil took it," added the girl. "But of nothing but flowers."

"And then *they* drove up, two new men in a car, no uniforms, and said Phil would have to be questioned. They said this to us in French. And they just—took him away."

"But that's incredible," cried Mrs. Pollifax. "Does the Embassy know?"

"We went there at once. It was a big shock to them. This morning they say he has been charged with espionage, and the Embassy suggests we leave this country at once," he said in a melancholy voice. "Because we were with him."

"Which we will do," added the French boy, "on the six o'clock plane out of Sofia this afternoon."

Debby said suddenly, "I think it's terrible just going

off and leaving Phil. It could have been any of us, and he's here all alone—"

"You heard Nikki. He's going to stay a few days and keep doing everything possible."

"Nikki's not leaving with you?" asked Mrs. Pollifax sharply.

She thought Debby looked at her appraisingly. "No," the girl said quietly. "How do you happen to know who Nikki is?"

"Philip complained about him."

"Yes," said Debby, looking abstracted.

The French boy had glanced at his watch. "We must go," he said. "We must be certain we catch that plane. It's nearly three o'clock now and we want to stop again at the Embassy for news." He looked politely at Mrs. Pollifax. "You have been kind to ask."

"But I'm terribly sorry," she said. "For all of you, but especially for Philip. You're quite sure you'll be allowed to leave safely?"

"Reasonably sure, madam," said the French boy. "We have the assurances of your Embassy."

Mrs. Pollifax nodded. "I'm glad."

Debby said politely, "We hope your stay is a pleasanter one than ours. You're at the Hotel Pliska?"

Mrs. Pollifax shook her head. "The Rila."

Debby nodded. "Good-bye. You've been nice to ask."

One by one they shook hands with her, and Mrs. Pollifax watched them move across the terrace trailing their packs behind them. She thought about Philip Trenda, remembering his thick black hair, the level blue eyes, his dysentery and his indecision over staying or going, and she felt very alarmed for him. A Bulgarian prison was hardly a fitting experience for such a young person. He probably didn't even know that his Embassy was trying to reach him. He would be feeling very alone, very frail, and of course almost no Bulgarians spoke English, which would make it all the more frustrating.

But espionage! Despite the warmth of the sun across her shoulders, Mrs. Pollifax shivered. There but for the grace of God, she reminded herself, and at that moment she glanced up and met the eyes of the little gray man in the gray suit. He looked hastily away, but his interest was no longer coincidence. *He's following me,* she thought. The bright terrace seemed dimmer and the breeze cold.

After a trip down and back on Mount Vitosha's cable car—it would have been exhilirating if she had not just learned of Philip's arrest—Mrs. Pollifax drove her rented car slowly back through the environs of Sofia and to her hotel. It was four o'clock when she picked up her key at the desk. She ascended in the elevator carrying half a dozen picture postcards to write, and was just settling down to them at the desk when she heard a light knocking at her door.

Tsanko at last! thought Mrs. Pollifax with relief, and hurried across the room to fling open the door.

A teary-eyed Debby stood in the hall.

"But—oh dear!" faltered Mrs. Pollifax.

The girl said defiantly, "I want to talk to you. I *have* to talk to you."

"But your plane—good heavens! Aren't you missing your plane?"

"I'm not taking the plane."

A chambermaid down the hall was watching them. Mrs. Pollifax said, "Come inside."

"They can arrest me if they want. I'm not leaving," stormed Debby as she followed Mrs. Pollifax into the room. "Not until Phil's free. I know Nikki said we all *must* get out quickly, but I can't. Phil's my friend, he's the nicest boy I ever met."

"But this isn't America, you know," Mrs. Pollifax said, closing the door and then locking it. "It may take weeks to free your young man." She looked at Debby, who had

thrown herself into the chair by the window, and after
one glance at the girl's clenched jaw she added quietly,
"There isn't anything you can *do,* you know."

"I can be suspicious," she said indignantly. "I tried
to talk to the others, Andre especially, but they told me
I was imagining things. They didn't *want* to listen."

Mrs. Pollifax said with interest, "Imagining what
things?"

"You'll say the same thing," the girl cried accusingly.
"You will, I know you will. But I won't get on the plane—
I won't."

"Then why did you come here?" asked Mrs. Pollifax.
"I remember how very casually you asked at what hotel
I was staying. You knew even then that you were going
to stay behind in Sofia and come here to see me. Why?"

"Because all of a sudden—for no reason at all—you
said, 'Nikki isn't leaving with you?' And you looked surprised. And that's it, you see—Nikki."

Mrs. Pollifax abruptly sat down on the edge of the
bed. "Nikki. . . . Go on."

Leaning forward, the girl said earnestly, "It's Nikki
who insisted we come to Bulgaria. Nobody—but nobody—
had the slightest intention of coming here, or even wanted
to. 'Let's go to Bulgaria' he said day after day, like brain-
washing, and it was Nikki who got the visas for us, he
handled everything. Phil didn't want to come. He said
Bulgaria was the last place he wanted to go. He had every
intention of not coming—"

"Yes, I know. Why did he let you all persuade him?"

Debby looked helplessly at Mrs. Pollifax. "It's crazy,
I know it is, but I think Phil was drugged."

Mrs. Pollifax started. "Drugged!"

She nodded. "Yes. From all that Phil said, he planned
to see the rest of us off on the plane and either wait for
us in Belgrade or go back to Dubrovnik. I mean, he really
wasn't going to *go* to Bulgaria."

"Yes," said Mrs. Pollifax in a startled voice, remembering.

"Nikki gave him a pill at breakfast that day—he said it was a dysentery pill. All I know is that Phil did get on that plane and he slept. He slept so hard that nobody could rouse him, nobody could talk to him and when we got to Sofia the stewardess had to help us wake him. And then . . ."

"Yes?"

Debby scowled. "That's only part of it. When we got to Customs, Nikki acted so strangely. It happened because he couldn't find something, some paper or other—it must have been paper because he kept turning his wallet inside out, and what will fit in a wallet except paper? The Customs man got very uptight about it all and he called some other man in uniform, who took us out of line, and he took Nikki away to question him. The other kids were afraid for Nikki, except . . ."

"Yes?"

She shook her head. "I got a different feeling. There was something wrong about it all. I don't know how to explain it except I've noticed in the communist countries how quiet people get when they meet a uniform. They're afraid of drawing attention to themselves, you know? It's spooky. But Nikki acted so—so arrogant. As if the Customs man was a peasant. Nikki wasn't afraid, he was *furious*."

Mrs. Pollifax was silent; it was not until Debby spoke again that she realized how far her thoughts had gone.

"Well?" asked Debby angrily. "You're going to tell me I'm crazy now, aren't you?"

Mrs. Pollifax looked at her and smiled. "Foolhardy, perhaps. Reckless to stay, yes. Crazy, no. You think Philip was persuaded into Bulgaria for just this purpose? To be arrested?"

Debby looked startled. "Is that what I think? I hadn't

followed it that far. I just don't think Nikki is what he appears to be."

Mrs. Pollifax nodded absently. She was thinking that this was clearly her moment of truth and that she had a decision to make. The sensible thing, of course, was to place Debby in a taxi and send her off at once, alone, to the American Embassy. There she would be listened to by a minor clerk, told that she had a lively imagination and shipped out of Sofia with dispatch.

That was the sensible course. Debby would be upset, but she would survive; Mrs. Pollifax would remain at leisure to carry out her courier assignment with no complications; Philip Trenda would eventually be released because surely American citizens couldn't be imprisoned forever on trumped-up charges? But the drawback to taking the sensible course, reflected Mrs. Pollifax, was that it so frequently diminished the people involved. Debby would survive but certainly not without suffering a deep loss of faith. She herself would remain at leisure, but at the cost of a lively quarrel with her conscience, and there was no one to guarantee Philip Trenda's freedom, or even his future. Not yet.

Mrs. Pollifax made the only decision that was possible for her. "If we hurry I think we can get to the Embassy before it closes," she said, and stood up. "I'll go with you. I think your doubts about Nikki are quite sound, for reasons which I'll explain when we get there."

"You mean you're listening?" gasped the girl.

"I'm listening," said Mrs. Pollifax. "You've already missed your plane. Have you any money? Have you a room for tonight?"

"Money, yes," said Debby. "No room, because we bunked in a place Nikki found for us and I didn't want him to know I was staying behind."

"Very shrewd of you," said Mrs. Pollifax, placing her hat squarely on her head. "If Rila has no space for you, you can share this room, but you really must promise to leave Sofia in the morning," she told her sharply. "You simply can't go around expressing yourself in a country like this without getting into a great deal of trouble."

"I'm already in trouble," Debby said forlornly.

"Then promise, and let's go."

9

It was almost six o'clock before they were ushered into the office of a Mr. Benjamin Eastlake at the Embassy. "I want you to listen to this young friend of Philip Trenda's," Mrs. Pollifax said, adding tartly, "if only because we've had to talk to so many people before reaching you. I shouldn't care to try finding you again."

"My apologies," Eastlake said. "I've been running late all day and now I'm overdue at a tiresome cocktail party. I'm well protected by secretaries," he added wryly. "A most serious business, this, the Bulgarians arresting an American and charging him with espionage. I've been in touch with Washington all day and I can tell you that a formal complaint has already been lodged with the Bulgarian government."

"Will that help?" asked Debby eagerly.

Eastlake shrugged. "It depends entirely on why the Bulgarians arrested him. Or why they *think* they arrested him."

"Perhaps what Debby would like to tell you may add a piece to the puzzle," suggested Mrs. Pollifax.

Eastlake smiled at Debby. "You look familiar. You were here yesterday?"

Debby smiled back shyly. "Yes, except I didn't say anything. Nikki did all the talking."

He nodded. "Very well. Talk."

Debby explained her suspicions to Mr. Eastlake, beginning with Belgrade and ending with her visit to Mrs. Pollifax at the Hotel Rila.

"Who quite wisely felt I should hear this," he said judiciously. "But you know it's very difficult to believe this young Nikki can be quite as sinister as you paint him. He was properly outraged about the whole situation, and extremely concerned."

Mrs. Pollifax said quietly, "I wonder if you know what passport he travels under?"

"Passport? You mean his nationality?" Eastlake rang a buzzer. "Bogen, could you get me that list of young people traveling with Trenda?" It was given him and as he glanced down the sheet he frowned. "Odd."

"What is?"

"He had a German passport. He didn't have a German accent."

"He told us he was Yugoslavian," Debby said indignantly.

Eastlake's scowl lightened. "Then he's probably a transplanted Yugoslavian. Yugoslavs are allowed to leave their country, you know. Theirs is the only communist government that allows immigration, free access and egress, et cetera." He smiled. "Very possible, you know, for him to be both German and Yugoslavian."

Mrs. Pollifax was not to be diverted. She said firmly, "Last night I went to the apartment of a gentleman I'd been told might become my guide around Sofia. Do you know a Mr. Carleton Bemish?"

Eastlake winced. "I've met him. I shouldn't care to *know* him."

"Mr. Bemish appeared to have met with a windfall,"

she continued quietly. "Champagne on the table. Boxes of new clothes on his couch. He wasn't at all interested in becoming my guide. He was far more interested in the guest he was expecting."

Eastlake looked bored but polite.

"As I was about to leave," she went on crisply, "his guest arrived at the door and they greeted one another effusively, like very old friends. His guest," she added, "was Nikki."

"Nikki!" echoed Eastlake.

"Nikki?" said Debby in a startled voice and turned to stare at Mrs. Pollifax in astonishment. "But Nikki's never been to Bulgaria before. He said so."

"Can you be certain it was Nikki?" asked Eastlake with a frown.

"I was so certain that I reminded him I'd seen him in the Belgrade air terminal, and had traveled on the same plane. He made no attempt to deny it. In fact we spoke of . . ." She stopped in mid-sentence.

"What?" asked Debby, leaning forward.

Mrs. Pollifax frowned. "I'd quite forgotten. I told him I'd seen you all being questioned at Customs, and I told Nikki I hoped there had been no trouble."

"Yes?" said Eastlake, no longer looking bored.

"Nikki said it had been nothing, only a small misunderstanding, but *he didn't mention that Philip had been arrested.*"

"This was last night?"

Mrs. Pollifax nodded.

"But that was hours after Phil had been arrested," gasped Debby. "What time?"

"About seven."

"Only an hour after Nikki was here in this office wanting to know what was being done to release Phil," said Eastlake. "You think Nikki could be Bulgarian?"

"It's an interesting possibility, don't you think?" suggested Mrs. Pollifax.

Eastlake whistled. "It would certainly put a different light on the subject."

Debby was looking excited. "Oh, I'm so glad we came!"

Mrs. Pollifax looked at her. "But none of this begins to free Philip, you know. It may only make it . . . more difficult."

"But why?"

It was Eastlake who replied. "She means that there may be some purpose behind Phil's arrest that we don't know and can't guess." He regarded Debby thoughtfully.

"What are you thinking?" asked Mrs. Pollifax, watching him. "What will you do?"

He lifted both hands helplessly. "Report this at once to Washington, of course."

"But why Phil?" asked Debby.

"Exactly. Why not you, or that young Andre? Why anybody at all?" asked Eastlake. "Above all, why a young American student? If they're trying to provoke an incident . . ." His lips tightened. "Now that you've reported this, Debby, I want your promise to be on the morning plane out of Sofia."

Debby sighed. "I already promised Mrs. Pollifax."

"Then if you'll wait in the corridor I'd like to speak to Mrs. Pollifax alone."

When she had gone Eastlake shook his head and stood up. He walked to the window, stared out and then turned. "A damnable situation," he growled. "That girl absolutely must be gotten out of Bulgaria tomorrow."

"You think she's in danger?"

He looked at her in surprise. "Danger? Not very likely. Why should she be?"

"I thought—"

"It has other ramifications," he said curtly. "I wish like hell this girl had left with the others. The Bulgarians are very strait-laced about their young people. I've been trying all day—before I heard these new details—to find out who on earth allowed these kids into this country."

"I don't understand," said Mrs. Pollifax.

"They're virtually hippies," he said bluntly. "Oh, nice enough kids, of course, but not representative of our best American youth. The propaganda value of their appearance alone is enough to turn my hair white. I understand they were seen walking barefooted in Sofia—and not a one of the young men has had a haircut in months."

"I see," said Mrs. Pollifax. "I suppose it's your job to consider things like this, but I would have thought you might be more concerned about—"

"Naturally I'm concerned," he snapped. "But I happen to officially represent the United States here and this means thinking in terms of image." He leaned forward. "I'm talking about publicity, Mrs. Pollifax, Photographs. Make sure that girl leaves tomorrow, and wearing shoes and a clean dress."

"I'm not sure she has a dress," said Mrs. Pollifax tartly. "She's waiting outside, do you want to ask her?"

He looked at her. "Just get her out before the news story heats up."

"In the meantime," said Mrs. Pollifax, rising, "I assume that you'll keep in mind that Philip Trenda, no matter what length his hair, is still an American citizen?"

Eastlake gave her a long, level scrutiny. "Oh yes, Mrs. Pollifax, we will," he said dryly. "We do our best for distressed American citizens even if they turn out to be criminals or bona fide spies. But it would be infinitely simpler if it was someone like yourself who had been arrested yesterday."

"Even if I turned out to be a spy?" asked Mrs. Pollifax with a pleasant smile.

He looked at her pityingly, as if the poverty of her humor overtaxed his patience, and Mrs. Pollifax left with the feeling that she had delivered the last word, even if her audience didn't realize it.

At nine she and Debby dined together in the hotel restaurant. They had no sooner ordered when a waiter emerged who spoke primitive English—Mrs. Pollifax wondered where the management had been hiding him—and announced that Balkantourist was calling her on the telephone at the front desk.

"That will be Nevena," she said with a sigh, and left Debby to follow the man upstairs to the lobby. "Mrs. Pollifax," she said into the phone.

But it was not Balkantourist. "How do you do," said a man's voice, lightly accented. "This is the man from the shop you visited yesterday. About the brown sheepskin vest?"

"Oh—yes," gasped Mrs. Pollifax. "Yes indeed." She was aware of two desk clerks at her elbow and she inched unobtrusively away from them. "I'm very glad to hear," she said, but of one thing she was certain: this was not the same man she had spoken with in the tailor shop—the voice and the accent were different.

"Our mutual friend has been called away," continued the voice smoothly. "It is suggested you meet him in Tarnovo."

"Where?"

"It is some distance. You have a car? It is suggested you leave tomorrow, Wednesday morning. It is a drive in miles of some one hundred fifty. A reservation has been made for you at the Hotel Yantra tomorrow night."

"Those two names," said Mrs. Pollifax, fumbling for a pencil. "Again, please?"

"Tarnovo. T-a-r-n-o-v-o. The Hotel Yantra."

"Yes," said Mrs. Pollifax, baffled by such unexpected instructions. "But why?" she asked. "Is this really necessary? I don't understand—"

The voice was cold. "Quite necessary." A gentle click at the other end of the line told her that she was no longer in contact with her mysterious caller. She placed the receiver back on the hook. With a polite smile for the two young desk clerks, she made her way quickly to the ladies' room, locked the door behind her and removed a map of Bulgaria from her purse. Eventually she found Tarnovo —it was the center of the country.

But why? she thought indignantly. Why must she leave Sofia and go driving halfway across Bulgaria, even if the country *was* only three hundred miles from west to east?

She could think of only two reasons at the moment. The small gray man might *not* be one of Tsanko's people. Or Shipkov's message and his telephone call were both a trap and there was no Tsanko at all.

Neither possibility was heartening. But she had come to Bulgaria to carry out an assignment and this was the first communication she'd received. If it was a trap, she was going to have to discover it for herself by following it through to the end.

Carefully she tore up her written notes on Tarnovo and flushed them down the toilet. Returning to Debby she said, "I'll be leaving Sofia too, tomorrow. I'm going to do a little touring of the countryside."

"Oh," said Debby, startled.

Mrs. Pollifax reached out and patted her hand. "But I won't forget about Philip. I'll keep in touch with the Embassy for as long as I'm in Bulgaria and if you'll give me your address I'll write every piece of news I hear."

But even as she reassured Debby she was thinking, Why Tarnovo? Why so far?

It was upsetting, and she admitted to a distinct uneasiness.

10

A change of plan was not casually accomplished. The hotel had collected Mrs. Pollifax's passport upon her arrival and in order to recover it she had to explain her plans to leave the next day. Balkantourist was telephoned, and an irate Nevena summoned again to demand what on earth she wanted.

"I want to drive into the country tomorrow and remain away for a few days," explained Mrs. Pollifax.

"You arrived only yesterday in Sofia."

"That's true. Now I want to leave."

"Why?"

Mrs. Pollifax sighed and embarked upon a story about meeting tourists that day who had told her Sofia was not the real Bulgaria.

"They said *that?*" Nevena said suspiciously. "Who were they?"

"I haven't the slightest idea. But in any case you know I want to see the real Bulgaria and I was planning anyway to drive into the country before I leave. Now I want to go tomorrow."

"Yes? Well, then, Borovets would be good, very good. It is south of Sofia, they ski there big in winter. I make a reservation at Hotel Balkantourist in Borovets for your arrival there tomorrow."

Mrs. Pollifax opened her mouth to protest and then closed it. There was obviously no point in mentioning Tarnovo to Nevena if Nevena wanted her to go to Borovets. If she persisted, the reservation at the Hotel Yantra might be accidentally uncovered, too. At this moment Mrs. Pollifax clearly understood the frustration that caused small children to lie through their teeth in the face of authority.

"Give me the manager, I speak with him," Nevena said, and Mrs. Pollifax gladly handed the phone to him. At length he promised to have her passport for her in the morning when she checked out.

"Thank you—nine o'clock," emphasized Mrs. Pollifax, and decided that it would be infinitely simpler if she did not mention that Debby would be staying the night with her.

Mrs. Pollifax set her alarm for a seven o'clock rising, determined to see that her young charge arrived at the airport on time; she wanted nothing to interfere with her new rendezvous in Tarnovo. She was pleased to note that at sight of a proper bathroom Debby made happy feminine sounds and dug out shampoo, soap and creams from her pack. It was possible, thought Mrs. Pollifax, that she would even wear a dress for the flight.

On this pleasant note Mrs. Pollifax fell asleep.

She awoke suddenly, with a rapidly beating heart. But this is growing tiresome, she thought, staring up at a man silhouetted beside her bed. He had half turned away from her and was holding an object up to the dim light from the window. He held it with one hand and with the other hand he stroked it. Eyes wide open now, Mrs. Pollifax saw that it was a knife he held. He was touching it, testing it, with a concentration that turned her cold.

He moved with infinite grace. His speed was incredible. Mrs. Pollifax barely had time to roll to the edge of the bed. As she dropped to the floor she heard the ugly ripping sound of the knife slicing the pillow where only a second before her head had lain. Then with a second swift movement he turned toward Debby's bed.

Mrs. Pollifax screamed.

It was a small scream, but it was effective. In the other bed Debby sat upright and turned on the bedside light in one fluid, competent motion that amazed Mrs. Pollifax. The light showed her assailant half-crouched between the beds, his eyes blinking at the sudden light.

Debby didn't scream. To Mrs. Pollifax's astonishment she stood up in bed and with a wild shout threw herself at the man and carried him to the floor with her. It was the most surprising tackle that Mrs. Pollifax had ever seen. The young, she thought, must feel so very un-used.

She stumbled to her feet to help. As Debby and the man rolled out into the middle of the room she saw the knife flash in the man's hand and abruptly he jumped to his feet. Debby clung to his legs. He viciously kicked away her grasp, brushed past Mrs. Pollifax, opened the door and fled.

Mrs. Pollifax had never seen him before. Since she was unlikely to see him again tonight she turned to Debby, who sat on the floor rocking back and forth in pain, her left hand cradled between her knees and blood streaming down her face from a scalp wound.

"Oh, my dear," gasped Mrs. Pollifax after one glance at the bone pushing its way through the skin of Debby's thumb and she hurried to the telephone. There she stopped, remembering that no one would understand her cry for help and that she'd already had a burglar the night before. She turned back. "Debby, we're going to have to get you downstairs to the lobby," she said fiercely.

"Can you walk? Your scalp wound needs stitches, and your thumb needs a splint."

"I'll be okay," Debby said in a dazed voice.

"Lean on me. And tell them you fell into a mirror, do you understand?"

"But he tried to kill me!" cried Debby.

Mrs. Pollifax nodded. "Yes," she said, and for just a moment allowed herself to remember what it had felt like to be inches away from his knife. But what troubled her most of all in remembering was that the man had known Debby was in the room with her. There'd been no hesitation at all—and no light shown—before he'd turned from Mrs. Pollifax to the next bed.

He had planned to murder them both.

"I don't think we can afford the police," she explained. "Trust me, will you?" Releasing Debby she hurried into the bathroom. The mirror lining the sink was impossible to fall into, but there was a full-length mirror attached to the back of the door. Mrs. Pollifax grabbed Debby's hairbrush and after several attacks succeeded in shattering the glass. "Let's go," she told Debby and they moved slowly out into the hall, a trail of blood taking shape behind them. The self-service elevator bore them down to the lobby, the doors slid open and Mrs. Pollifax carried her bloody companion into the lobby.

The picture they made abolished any need for translations. The desk clerk shouted, rang bells, pressed buzzers; a potential hotel scandal provoked the same reaction in any language and any country. Debby was delivered into the hands of a doctor who arrived breathless and beltless and still in bedroom slippers. The manager of the hotel followed, and then at last a representative of Balkantourist—but not Nevena, for which Mrs. Pollifax could be grateful.

It was daylight before it was all over: the setting and bandaging of Debby's thumb, the stitching of the scalp wound and the questions. It no longer mattered to Mrs.

Pollifax how it had all happened. What began to matter very much was her departure for Tarnovo in several hours; this was, after all, the whole point of her being in Bulgaria. "I want to speak," she told the Balkantourist representative firmly.

"Yes?"

"I am due to leave Sofia this morning in my car."

"Yes, yes, they have your passport ready to give you," he said.

"And the girl is to leave Sofia by plane this morning—"

"No," said the Balkantourist representative flatly.

"I beg your pardon?"

"The doctor says *no*. The doctor is firm. The girl cannot take flight alone. She must be looked after twenty-four hours. She is tired—spent, you know? There is some shock. To wander alone"—he shook his head disapprovingly—"she would cry, maybe faint, go unconscious. She needs the comfort of a presence, you understand?"

Mrs. Pollifax considered this; he was only too right, of course, but she couldn't possibly delay her own departure. Yet if she couldn't leave Debby here alone then there was only one alternative, and this dismayed her because she had no idea what lay ahead of her in Tarnovo. "Is she well enough to do a little driving in a car? In my *presence?*"

This was queried of the doctor, who smiled warmly, nodding. Mr. Eastlake wouldn't like this, she thought, but then Mr. Eastlake could be prevented from knowing about it. Tsanko wouldn't like it either—if they ever made contact—and she was sure that Carstairs would be appalled.

But she could scarcely abandon the child to a lonely hotel room for several days, and she could certainly not insist that Debby fly off to another lonely hotel room in another strange country. Her limitations as a ruthless agent had never been so pressing. Mrs. Pollifax sighed over them even as she said, "Good. She'll go with me then."

Everyone looked extremely relieved, and Mrs. Pollifax realized that the hotel would be delighted to be rid of her. Just to be sure of this she asked that a basket of fruit be packed for their drive, and two breakfasts be sent to her room.

It was exactly half-past nine when they drove away from the hotel, and considering the obstacles they'd encountered, Mrs. Pollifax congratulated herself on their leaving at all. Debby was curled up in the rear seat with orders to read road signs, remain quiet and stay warm. In any case Mrs. Pollifax had to concentrate for the first half an hour on getting them out of Sofia, with its maze-like streets leading into broad boulevards whose names all seemed to end in *ev* or *iski*. It was made more difficult by the fact that she wanted to go east on Route One toward Tarnovo, but she had been given detailed directions south, into artery number five, which would take her to Borovets. She was aware by this time of how few people spoke English in Bulgaria—and the perils of getting lost under such conditions—and so she simply followed her printed directions out of Sofia and then detoured north to Route One through a town called—incongruously—Elin Pelin. But all of this added miles to their excursion.

"There—we have reached Route One at last," she announced as they bounced onto a paved road. "Thank heaven that route numbers look the same in any language."

"Route One doesn't *feel* any better," Debby said, sitting up and looking around her. "What are these roads built of?"

Poplars lined the road, and beyond them stretched fields that carried the eye to the mountains on either side, still clouded by morning haze. The valley was green and rolling, punctuated by tidy haystacks at symmetrical intervals, and here and there low-lying walls of intricately worked stone. They passed a hay wagon and a farm truck and then no one.

"Of stone," said Mrs. Pollifax in reply. "Rather like those farm walls. You can see it here and there where the macadam's missing—a parquet affect." Waving a hand toward the mountains on their left, she added, "We cross that range further along, at Shipka Pass, where something like twenty-eight thousand Bulgarians died fighting the Turks."

"Twenty-eight *thousand?*" repeated Debby disbelievingly.

"You'll find it on the back of the map, translated into French, German and English. It says there's a monument and a restaurant there. They fought in the dead of winter and when they ran out of ammunition they threw rocks and boulders down the slopes at the Turks. There were eighteen survivors."

Debby whistled. "That beats Custer's last stand. Twenty-eight thousand and they didn't even *win?*"

"I don't think they're on the winning side very often in Bulgaria," said Mrs. Pollifax tartly.

Debby said, "That's dramatic, you know? I never thought about the places I hiked through this summer."

"Rather a waste. What *did* you think about?"

"Finding other kids. Looking for a piece of the action. That sort of thing."

"Do your parents know you just wander about picking up rides and people?"

Debby emitted a sound like *"Ech."*

"Do they even know you're in *Bulgaria?*" she asked in a startled voice.

This time Debby's comment sounded like *"Aaaah."*

Mrs. Pollifax sighed. "Debby, if we're going to be traveling together I really think you'll have to enlarge your vocabulary. I'm sure you'd much prefer to be with people your own age, but for a few days we'll have to accept this situation and lay down some ground rules. Later you can explain what *'aaaah'* means, but what on earth is *'ech'?*"

Debby looked resentful. "Dr. Kidd doesn't ask things like that. He's my psychiatrist and he wants me to be spontaneous."

"Well, I've nothing against psychiatrists or spontaneity," retorted Mrs. Pollifax, "but I do think clear communication simplifies life a great deal. Now. What does *ech* mean?"

Debby laughed. "It sounds so funny when you say it."

"It sounds funny when you say it, too. What took you to a psychiatrist, by the way?"

"I run away a lot," Debby said vaguely. "And I get attached to too many boys. It upsets my parents. Dr. Kidd says I get devoted to people because *they're* not. Dr. Kidd says they are, but I don't believe it. How *can* they be when they never say no and are scared of me?"

Mrs. Pollifax deftly supplied her own translation. "You mean you haven't written your parents at all since you left America?"

"That's right," said Debby. "I'm giving them a restful summer."

"But don't they mind not hearing? Don't they worry?"

"You know," she said a little wistfully, "I wish they did sometimes. Just once in a while. They really don't know what to do with me and they always want me to be *happy.* I'm too old for summer camps now so they said I could go to Europe on my own. Dr. Kidd said maybe I'll find myself by doing it."

Mrs. Pollifax was silent and then she said lightly, dryly, "I see. Rather like a lost-and-found department."

But Debby had grown tired of the subject. "I wonder how Phil is today. What's at this Borovets place we're going to visit, or are you going to say I'll find out soon enough?"

"You would if we were going there," Mrs. Pollifax told her. "But we're not, we're going to Tarnovo."

"For Pete's sake why?"

"Because I've never had any intention of going anywhere else," said Mrs. Pollifax reasonably. "Debby, look at the map and see if there's a gas station at Zlatica, will you? You'll find tiny red automobiles printed on the map wherever one can buy gas."

Debby rustled the map. "Yes, there's one at Zlatica. Isn't it weird? There aren't many in the whole country. Or cars either."

Mrs. Pollifax said without expression, "There's been a black Renault behind us on the road for some time. I think we'll have the gas tank filled and let it pass us." She'd first noted the car as far back as Elin Pelin, because of the clouds of dust it had raised behind them on that particular stretch of dusty countryside. Now, some miles later, it was still there and the coincidence made her uneasy.

Near Zlatica she pulled into the neat cement and grass compound decorated with flower beds and Nempon signs, and two husky women in blue overalls emerged.

"Oh, wow," said Debby, collapsing into giggles.

"Sssh," said Mrs. Pollifax, sternly, and after a clumsy exchange of sign language and a great number of titters and smiles, the gas tank was filled, the oil checked and bills counted. More important, the black Renault passed them and disappeared ahead.

The road carried them along the floor of the valley, the mountains on either side growing sharper as the haze cleared. They passed tiny thatch-roofed farmhouses, each with its yard neatly enclosed by fences made of woven twigs. Sometimes an old woman sat on a bench by the door, a spindle in one hand, a bundle of flax in the other. Once they saw a shepherd standing at a distance on a hill, his watchtower behind him, a marvelous leather cape across his shoulders. "He actually carries a *crook*," Debby said in awe.

And then the fields turned into acre after acre of roses, entire hillsides dotted with extravagant pinks and yellows and scarlets. "This must be the Valley of Roses," Debby announced after a look at the map.

"Debby, I'm thinking about that horrid man with the knife last night," said Mrs. Pollifax abruptly. "Where did you learn to tackle like that, by the way? You were marvelous."

"Oh that was nothing," Debby said eagerly. "You should see me on the parallel bars and the ropes. I adore phys. ed., it's the only subject I pass in school. What about that man? Do you think he had anything to do with Phil's arrest?"

"I don't know," said Mrs. Pollifax honestly. "Debby, have you any idea at all why it should have been Philip who was arrested?"

"Of course not," said Debby. "I wish we could stop at one of those rose places. Want a grape from the basket?"

"No, and you answered my question much too quickly," she said. "Of course the answer wouldn't be obvious. Tell me what you know about him."

"About Phil?" Debby was smiling. "Nothing much except I think he's just great. He digs Simon and Garfunkel —and Leonard Cohen—and he's gentle and he *listens*."

"Debby."

"Hmm?"

"I didn't ask how you *feel* about him, I'm trying to find out why he was arrested for espionage an hour after he arrived in Bulgaria. Facts."

"Facts?" echoed Debby blankly.

"Yes, for instance, where does Philip come from? Where does he live? What do his parents do?" Mrs. Pollifax glanced into the rearview mirror at Debby's face and saw its bewilderment.

"Oh. Well . . ." Debby began, and floundered. "I only met him three weeks ago," she said indignantly. *"Those* things don't matter."

"They matter now," said Mrs. Pollifax firmly. "Think. Concentrate."

"If you want *labels*," Debby said scornfully, "he's a sophomore at the University of Illinois."

"Good! An excellent beginning." She realized that she was asking Debby to violate an unspoken code and she added very gently, "It's this sort of thing, Debby, that could solve the riddle. More, it could help free him."

Debby said promptly, "Well, I've got some of his books in my pack. Maybe he scribbled his address in one of them."

Mrs. Pollifax heard rustlings and clankings and smiled as she saw Debby toss out a tin drinking cup, a hairbrush and an assortment of paperbacks. Debby said, "This one's his—and this—and the Kahlil Gibran. Hey," she shouted, "I found something."

"Hooray," said Mrs. Pollifax.

"It was stuck in the pages as a bookmark." She handed Mrs. Pollifax a pocket calendar the size of a playing card, a familiar plasticized type distributed by banks and corporations at Christmastime.

Mrs. Pollifax handed it back. "Read it to me," she said. "I can't read it without stopping the car."

"It says"—Debby held it up to the light—"in large letters it says TRENDA-ARCTIC OIL COMPANY, and under this in small letters, *President, Peter F. Trenda, Headquarters Chicago, Illinois; Fairbanks, Alaska, and St. John's, Newfoundland.*"

Mrs. Pollifax nodded. "Good for you. I feel better."

Debby's voice was disappointed. "All it means is that Phil's parents are rich. Filthy rich, possibly."

Mrs. Pollifax glanced into the rearview mirror at Debby. "Even that's a help," she told her, and then her glance went beyond Debby to the road. A black Renault sedan had just driven out of a side road and was driving at some distance behind them.

11

The reached Shipka Pass shortly after noon, having
stopped a few minutes to marvel at the Shipka Monastery,
with its gold onion domes gleaming softly in the sun like
an enchanted fairy-tale palace.

Once at the summit they parked the car in the broad
flat parking area and Mrs. Pollifax stood a minute listening to the wind. "It sounds like the sea," she said. "As if
it's swept thousands and thousands of miles without meeting any resistance." She realized that she was also listening for the sound of an engine behind them, and when no
black Renault appeared she sighed with relief. Turning
toward the low stone buildings she said, "Let's treat
ourselves to a really Bulgarian lunch, shall we?"

"Great," said Debby. "How far are we from that place
you want to go?"

"About twenty or thirty miles. Not far."

They lunched on cuzek patladjan and mishmash and
misquette grapes under dark murals of the Battle of
Shipka Pass. Mrs. Pollifax produced aspirin from her bag
for Debby, whose thumb was beginning to throb, and

they bought a few postcards in the lobby. While Debby lingered in the ladies' room Mrs. Pollifax wandered outside just in time to see a black Renault sedan drive out of the parking expanse and head down the mountain toward Gabrovo and Tarnovo.

She watched it vanish with a worried frown. It was possible that another tourist might drive from Sofia to Shipka Pass along this same route, and at precisely the same hour, but it struck her as exceedingly odd that they reached Shipka Pass at the same time. She had stopped for gas at Zlatica, and had seen the Renault pass them, and then they had stopped at the monastery and had again seen the Renault pass. Yet the Renault had not reached the summit before they did, and now it was just leaving.

If that's the same Renault, then we're being followed, she thought, naming her fear. But by whom? There had been the small gray man in the gray suit, her mysterious burglar of the first evening, the man with the knife last night, and there was the remote possibility that Tsanko could be keeping them under surveillance. She couldn't imagine Balkantourist going to such lengths to make sure that she reached Borovets. Remembering Nevena's character, she thought that Balkantourist would have flagged her down two miles out of Sofia and sternly forced her back on the road southward.

I don't like it, she thought, remembering that she was here on nothing but faith and a telephone call from a stranger. It was extraordinary, this abrupt order to leave Sofia and drive halfway across Bulgaria. Could Tsanko really be trusted?

She felt acutely lonely as she stood listening to the sound of the wind. Her only companion was a charming, waif-like child who was more likely to prove a liability in case of untoward circumstances. She herself felt unaccountably frail. She thought it must stem from the odd juxtaposition of the familiar and the sinister; no country so foreign in nature had the right to look so much like the American countryside of New England, with Queen Anne's lace growing along the roads, poplar trees and spruces thickly lining the slopes, and mountains scalloping the horizon at a distance. It was *not* New England, but its very familiarity blunted all sense of real danger. She had to struggle to remember that this was a police state and a country where almost no English was spoken. What was most provoking of all, the words were so cluttered with consonants that one couldn't even guess their meaning. What *could* one do with a word spelled СВЯТ?

"Hey—what's the matter?" asked Debby, joining her, "You look spooky."

"I *feel* spooky," admitted Mrs. Pollifax with a frown. "I don't know why, either, except I have the feeling we shouldn't have stopped here for lunch."

"It must be the ghosts of Shipka Pass," Debby said. "You know—those twenty-eight thousand Bulgarians killed here fighting the Turks."

"Of course," said Mrs. Pollifax lightly. "Shall we go now?"

They had traveled only a few miles down the mountainside when the brakes failed. The road was steep and curving, with a precipitous drop on the right and a precipitous slope on the left. As Mrs. Pollifax stamped helplessly on the brake pedal again and again the car only gathered momentum. Furiously she tugged at the emergency brake; for just a second it caught, lessening their speed, and then the emergency snapped under the strain and came away in her hand.

"What is it?" cried Debby.

"Brakes," gasped Mrs. Pollifax, and clung to the wheel as they gathered speed and wildly careened around a hairpin curve. Out of the corner of her eye she saw the sheer, cliff-like drop on their right. Nothing on earth could hold their wheels on the road if they met a second curve like this. They would fly off the mountain into space and plummet to the depths of the ravine.

"We've got to crash," she shouted. "Get down!"

The road briefly straightened. With all of her strength Mrs. Pollifax leaned on the steering wheel, pulling it toward the mountain side of the road. Every instinct in her body fought a crash. The wall of the mountain loomed near to the windshield and for just one second she stared straight into rich black soil lightly covered over with low evergreens, grass, the stunted trunk of a tree in a crevice, and then came the impact of metal against earth, terrible grinding noises, the splintering of glass and silence.

She opened her eyes to discover that she was still alive. "Debby?" she gasped.

From somewhere behind her Debby mumbled something unintelligible and her head lifted from the floor of the car. "I'm okay," she said in a surprised voice. A second later she added with still more surprise, "But I think I'm going to scream if we don't get out of here. Are we trapped?"

Mrs. Pollifax looked around her. The car had tunneled its way several feet into the steep hillside—she shuddered to think how fast they'd been going—and she was staring into a wall of earth. "We'll break the back window," she announced. "Open up the rear seat, they said the tools are under it." Her hat was on the floor; she picked it up and placed it on her head again.

A few minutes later the last surviving window of the car had been broken with a lug, and Debby threw out her pack and crawled after it. Mrs. Pollifax followed less gracefully with her suitcase and sat down beside her next to the road. She realized that her hands were trembling badly, and she pressed them together in her lap. I hope I'm not going to faint, she thought.

"Well, are you going to sue the Volkswagen people or Balkantourist?" asked Debby indignantly. "We could have been *killed!*"

A dozen replies occurred to Mrs. Pollifax, all of which she discarded. It didn't seem the kindest moment to tell Debby that their brakes must have been tampered with while they lunched at Shipka Pass. It was a miracle they were still alive.

She thought, I'll tell her later, and she wished with surprising savagery that Debby had left on the plane this morning, broken thumb or no, for it was even less pleasant to realize it might be Debby someone was determined to murder.

Within the hour they caught a lift with a farmer who spoke no English but who nevertheless managed to express his genuine horror over their plight. He placed them in his battered truck, offered them peaches and cigarettes and drove them to Gabrovo. But not to a Nempon station; he took them to the police.

Well, thought Mrs. Pollifax philosophically, in for a penny, in for a pound.

The houses in Gabrovo were the same dun-colored stucco boxes they had seen along the way, the roofs of clay tile or thatch, the windows curtained with yellowing newspapers. The police, however, were quartered behind a wall with a gate, over which was suspended a neat black sign. From the main building just inside the gate jutted long low buildings forming a perfect square around a compound of grass and flowers in the center. Their Bulgarian friend went inside and came out with two policemen in uniforms of dark trousers and apple-green Eisenhower jackets. Presumably he had explained the condition of their car and its abandonment. Passports were shown, and after a brief interval another farmer was summoned who spoke some English—he had once worked a year in Kansas, he said—and he reported that the police were heartbroken at the situation of the American tourists. The proper authorities would be notified, the car towed to the nearest Nempon station and a message conveyed to them in Tarnovo when repairs had been made.

In the meantime—with the apologies of everyone concerned—there was nothing in town for them with wheels except a motorcycle.

"Motorcycle?" said Mrs. Pollifax doubtfully.

"Oh beautiful," cried Debby ecstatically. "I know how to drive a motorcycle, I ride one lots of times at home."

It was in this way that Mrs. Pollifax and Debby roared into Tarnovo on a motorcycle with Debby at the handlebars, the luggage roped to the rear and Mrs. Pollifax squashed between them, one hand inside of Debby's belt, the other clinging to her hat.

12

Nothing had prepared Mrs. Pollifax for Tarnovo. It was built all over six hilltops of the Balkan mountain range and then repeatedly severed by the knife-cut wound of the Yantra's deep gorges. Houses tilted absurdly on the edge of the cliffs, and at the base–far below–trickled the Yantra, reduced by time and drought until its stream barely covered the bones of its riverbed. The old town, isolated, seemed to brush the sky and the clouds. It had once been the capital of an ancient kingdom–the Second Bulgarian Kingdom–and the remains of its fortress still crenelated the top of Tsaravets Hill. A stone entrance gate connected Tsaravets Hill to the main street of the town. This gate had stood since A.D. 1185, the only means of reaching a fortress rendered almost inviolate by the river encircling its hill half a mile below.

The Hotel Yantra was a modest building on a steep, cobblestoned street. Inside the open front door of the hotel lay a dusty lobby with a dusty leather couch and a glass-fronted display case of souvenirs: costumed dolls;

postcards; a few tubes of toothpaste, and cigarettes, including a dusty package of Camels.

"Pollifax," she said to the woman behind the desk.

The woman offered pencil and paper with which Mrs. Pollifax obligingly wrote her name. The woman studied it and gave a sharp cry of recognition. She rang a bell, reached for a key and handed it to her along with a large white envelope.

Mrs. Pollifax opened the envelope and drew out a sheet of unsigned notepaper. On it was typed:

> *Tsaravets Hill is charming by moonlight. About 10* P.M. *this evening, somewhere between gate and fortress.*

Her heart beat a little faster at the message; she crushed the paper into her purse and turned back to the woman, who had reverted to sign language. Matching her gestures, Mrs. Pollifax described Debby's need for lodging, too. Passports were submitted and they were shown to a room with two beds on the second floor.

"Again no screens," commented Mrs. Pollifax, standing at the open window. Their room was directly over the front door and the cobblestoned street. She could understand why defenestration was the most customary form of assassination in the Balkans—there had been no screens in Sofia, either and her room had been on the sixth floor.

"There's no water," called Debby from the bathroom.

"Nonsense, there has to be water," said Mrs. Pollifax, joining her. The floor of the tiny bathroom was painted a bilious green. There was neither tub nor shower stall, but high on one wall hung a shower spray with a drain under it. But none of the faucets yielded water. "I'll go and tell them," she said, and turned on her heel.

This challenge Mrs. Pollifax met by standing in front of the woman at the desk, wrenching open imaginary faucets and lifting her hands in dismay. The woman smiled and went to the telephone. A moment later she handed the receiver across the counter, gesturing to her to speak. "Hello?" Mrs. Pollifax said doubtfully.

"Yes," answered a voice at the other end of the wire. "You the English speak?"

"I certainly do," cried Mrs. Pollifax. "To whom am I speaking?"

"To Herr Vogel at Balkantourist hotel the street down. I visit here, some English I speak. The problem is what, *bitte?*"

"The problem is no water. Can you explain this to them here?"

"Ah . . ." The sigh was long and heavy. "But water there is nowhere at this hour, Fraulein. Between six and eight at night flows the water, you understand? Six and eight. In the morning flows the water seven to ten."

"Let me write that down," said Mrs. Pollifax despairingly. "But why the water flows—I mean, why?"

"A mountain town is Tarnovo, very high. Scarce is the water here. Did you see the jugs in the bathroom?"

"Jugs—yes."

"You the water fill with them, *bitte?* Six o'clock."

Mrs. Pollifax profusely thanked him, congratulated the clerk on her resourcefulness and went back to explain the situation to Debby, who was incredulous.

"It's ten minutes before six now," Mrs. Pollifax said. "I suggest we wait."

Precisely at six there issued from the bathroom an assortment of hollow noises, belches, rumbles and at last a trickling of water. Ten minutes later the toilet could be flushed. By that time Debby was at the sink washing a shirt and Mrs. Pollifax filling jugs of water, after which they took turns showering. They dined downstairs, below street level on an open balcony overlooking the gorge, and after this strolled briefly through the streets of the old town.

Shortly after nine o'clock Debby went to bed pleading exhaustion, and after reading a little while in the lobby

Mrs. Pollifax left the hotel to enter Tsaravets Gate.

Debby awoke reluctantly from her sleep and for a moment had no idea where she was. Oh yes, Bulgaria, she remembered, and then, Tarnovo, and then she remembered Mrs. Pollifax. What had awakened her was the sound of men talking under her window, and since the window was wide open, and the entrance to the hotel directly below her, the voices rang out loud and clear. She thought what a queer, primitive place it was: no air conditioning, no screens and water only a few hours a day. It was like entering another world through a time capsule.

She had not been asleep for long because it was still not dark—twilight, actually. Debby crawled out of bed and went to the window and stood there, wishing she dared lean out, perhaps even to ask the men below to tell their local jokes somewhere else. But she didn't feel particularly venturesome. She was tired and her thumb ached and it was pleasant to stand there looking out and feel a faint breeze enter the stifling room. There was a streetlamp across the cobblestoned pavement and under it a flower stand that was closing for the night. The old woman placed the flowers carefully in baskets—there were not many—and simply walked away. She thought it must be peaceful to live in a place like this and know who you were, know your roots and feel them grow deep. It was almost ten o'clock by Debby's travel clock and she wondered where Mrs. Pollifax had gone.

About Mrs. Pollifax Debby felt wary and a little threatened; wary because she didn't understand her and threatened because she was in danger of liking her very much. Such a thought appalled her. Debby had long ago stopped trusting adults and it followed that they had long since given up trusting her. Nor was she trustworthy in the least—Debby was the first to concede this—except with those of her own age, and her trust here was ardent, inviolate and usually misplaced, as Dr. Kidd made a point of reminding her.

But then Dr. Kidd was adult, too, and just a shade phony, his hair worn too self-consciously long, his clothes carefully mod.

Her problem with Mrs. Pollifax was that she couldn't find anything phony about her yet. She said exactly what she thought. She didn't make the slightest pretense at entertaining Debby or deferring to her. *We have to accept the situation and lay down some ground rules,* she'd said, and that was that. There seemed to be something infinitely *reliable* about her; it was incredible in anyone so Establishment. There was also the matter of the motorcycle, ridden without any trauma at all, and after the burglary Mrs. Pollifax had actually broken the mirror in the bathroom, which implied a cooler head than one might expect from a woman who wore a bird's nest on her head.

Now she was out walking somewhere instead of fussing over Debby and her broken thumb. It upset all of Debby's conclusions that adults lived dreary lives pleasing everyone except themselves and never having any fun.

The men under her window suddenly broke into loud laughter and departed. Twilight was slipping level by level into darkness and the solitary streetlamp brightened as the natural light retreated. A large open farm truck drove down the street, its brakes squealing. It was filled with women seated motionless all around the open sides, black silhouettes in shawls, patient stoic figures being taken off to work in the fields. There was something sinister about their stillness.

Hearing footsteps outside in the hall, Debby jumped back into bed and closed her eyes, not wanting Mrs. Pollifax to know she'd been missed. Her haste proved unnecessary, however, because Mrs. Pollifax seemed to be having a great deal of trouble with the lock and the key.

The door opened. Debby closed her eyes again and feigned sleep. This was a mistake because just as it dawned upon her that Mrs. Pollifax didn't wear heavy boots or smell of onions a pair of rough hands had stuffed a gag into her mouth. There wasn't even time to roll over and kick, or jump up and flail with her fists, because she found herself being rolled into a coarse, smelly rug—over and over—and then she was lifted up and—it was incredible but there was no other explanation—lifted to the open window and dropped into another pair of hands waiting below in the street.

It had grown abruptly dark as Mrs. Pollifax began her walk toward the fortress and she hugged her coat against the dampness and the mountain breeze. Crossing the bridge, she left behind the pleasant, companionable sounds of the town and entered a strange world of country silence. There were no lights along the narrow road. Ahead of her the moon rose over Tsaravets Hill outlining the lonely towers of the old fortress and for just a moment time turned itself upside down so that Mrs. Pollifax could imagine this same scene eight centuries ago: the wind blowing through the river gorge and up across the hills; the night watch on Baldwin Tower ready to challenge her approach; lanterns like fireflies moving through the distant fortress; the sound of horses' hoofs on cobbles, the sentry singing out the hour in whatever language they spoke in Byzantine days, and over it all the same timeless moon dusting the same dark feudal hills where tsars and patriarchs and boyars sharpened their swords and prayed to their saints for protection.

Ahead an owl hooted, and Mrs. Pollifax jumped. From among the shrubs and bushes on the hill came a girl's coquettish laugh followed by a small delighted scream. She was not entirely alone, realized Mrs. Pollifax, but still she turned and uneasily looked behind her.

A car was inching its way through Tsaravets Gate. In

the darkness it looked like a dark, moving slug with dim eyes. Its presence surprised her because she'd assumed the ancient gate was closed to traffic, and certainly not many cars existed that were small enough to drive through it. On the other hand she supposed that the officials involved in restoring the fortress had to have some means of entering. She stood back against the retaining wall that hugged the hill, and waited for the car to pass.

The car did not pass. It slowed as it neared her and then stopped. A door was opened, pinning her against the stone wall, and a voice said, "Get in, Mrs. Pollifax."

The voice astonished Mrs. Pollifax. "Mr.—*Bemish?*" she gasped, peering into the dark car. Surely Mr. Bemish couldn't be Tsanko! "Is that your voice, Mr. Bemish?" she asked uncertainly.

From the rear seat came sounds of movement, a stifled groan and then a shout: "Mrs. Pollifax! Run!"

"Debby?" gasped Mrs. Pollifax.

Before she could make sense of this—of Debby being in the car when less than an hour ago she had been sound asleep in the hotel, and of Mr. Bemish being here when he ought to be in Sofia—an arm reached out from the back seat and roughly pulled Mrs. Pollifax inside. The motor was gunned and the car jerked forward.

"How dare you!" cried Mrs. Pollifax, pummeling the driver's shoulders with her fists.

"Get her off me! Gag the girl!" shouted Bemish, and spoke sharply in Bulgarian to his companion, who caught Mrs. Pollifax's arms and pressed a revolver to the back of her neck. At the same time what had seemed to be a rolled-up rug on the floor of the car began to move, clumsily kicking Mrs. Pollifax. She lifted her feet.

"How did you get Debby?" she demanded of Bemish.

He chuckled. "Very simple, really. Yugov picked the lock of your room, rolled her into a rug and dropped her out of the window into my arms. These things are very casually done in the Balkans."

"But what on earth do you want of us?"

"You have made so much trouble, the two of you," he said simply. "It has to stop."

"What trouble?" she demanded. "You're kidnaping us and we don't even know why. I don't understand." Apparently no one cared to explain further and when she spoke again it was in a different voice. "May I ask where we're going?"

"To the fortress," said Bemish. "There are a number of excavations and pits honey-combing the area."

Excavations, pits—she did not like the sound of such words; they had a lonely, hollow ring to them. Nor did Debby apparently, either, for she made a renewed effort to roll herself out of the rug. "Does Debby *have* to be tied up like an animal?" she asked quietly.

"Yes—like an animal," Bemish said. The hatred in his voice was almost a physical assault.

The car's headlights picked out an end to the retaining wall and a widening of the road into a cleared section. Above them the horizon was occupied by the outline of the fortress's tower and she realized they were almost under it. The car's lights were switched off and Mr. Bemish climbed out and turned. He held a gun in his hand; this much the moon illuminated. "Out," he said, waving the gun.

"I don't want to get out," said Mrs. Pollifax.

"Out, or I'll shoot the girl here and now."

Mrs. Pollifax climbed out.

"This way," Bemish said, prodding her. His companion followed, carrying Debby wrapped in the rug over his shoulder. After walking a few paces Bemish drew apart a clump of bushes and descended rock steps into a hole that was half cellar, half excavation. The man behind Mrs. Pollifax trod on her heel and then shoved her down as well. She entered what appeared to be the corner of an ancient, half-buried room.

Bemish was lighting a candle. "Over there," he said

curtly, his face washed clean of friendliness. He brought a smaller gun from his jacket and began attaching a silencer to it, taking his time.

Mrs. Pollifax thought, There must be something I can do or say. She felt curiously mesmerized, completely unable to come to grips with their seizure. It had all happened so quickly. She had faced death before on her other assignments, but her protestations of innocence had never been so genuine as they were now. The moment seemed totally unreal—insane—because of its senselessness. "Why?" she said aloud to Bemish, and then as his companion unrolled Debby from the rug and propped her up beside Mrs. Pollifax, she said furiously, "You've made a terrible mistake! It's unspeakable, your murdering an innocent girl like this!"

"Orders," Bemish said, tight-lipped.

"From whom? And why?"

He looked at her closely. "You make nothing but trouble, Mrs. Pollifax, and now you make questions. You think I risk your speaking just once more with Mr. Eastlake?"

"Eastlake!" she gasped. "But that was about Philip!"

His lips trembled; drops of sweat shone on his forehead. "Bulgaria is my home now—my home, do you know what that means?" he shouted at her. "There's nowhere left for me to go, and you stick your silly American noses into my business. There's big money at stake, months of arrangements—months, do you hear?—and you come along and blunder into my business."

"*What* arrangements?" cried Mrs. Pollifax. "*What* money? *What* business?"

"Nikki understood," he shouted furiously. "Nikki saw right away that it's not fair. I've nothing, and Stella's brother has everything. If Petrov hadn't emigrated to America he'd have to share all his money, wouldn't he? He'd be forced to—this is a socialist country!"

He was plainly on the verge of hysteria. She felt pity for the violence in him that was driving him toward madness. Very quietly, for she had to understand, Mrs. Pollifax said, "Who is Stella, Mr. Bemish?"

"Stella? My wife, of course. And he sends her only hand-outs–his own sister!–when he has millions. Think of it, millions, and all in American dollars. Nikki understood, he saw immediately how unjust it is." Desperately he cried, "You think I want to kill you in cold blood like this? Don't you understand I have to, that it's orders? I must!"

His eyes widened in sudden astonishment. He said "orders" in a dazed voice, and then "must." His lips formed a silent O from which a trickle of blood emerged. Slowly, gently, he sank to the earth, his eyes fixed upon Mrs. Pollifax uncomprehendingly. His companion gasped and jumped for Bemish's fallen gun. As he reached it Mrs. Pollifax heard a soft *plop* and he, too, sank to the earth.

She stared in astonishment. They were both dead. Incredulous, she turned toward the entrance–to the gaping hole in the stone wall–and saw movement. Two men slid feet first into the cellar carrying rifles. One was young, dark and swarthy, wearing heavy corduroys and a gray sweater. The other man was Mrs. Pollifax's age, broad and bulky-shouldered with curling ironic brows. He said sharply to her, "You are Mrs. Pollifax?"

"Thank God," she gasped, suddenly weak.

"I'm Tsanko."

"Tsanko," she repeated numbly. "I'd almost forgotten. It wasn't a wild goose chase after all, then–you really are Tsanko!"

"*Da.*" He was kneeling beside the two men, searching them, and as he opened the wallet of Bemish's companion he whistled. "This one is a member of the secret police." He looked at Mrs. Pollifax questioningly and then his glance fell on Debby. "Your friend is still with gag," he said. "You wish this?"

Mutely, Mrs. Pollifax shook her head. She tugged at Debby's gag and at once the girl burst into tears. "I want to go home," she cried indignantly. "I don't like this country. Burglars, lousy brakes, Phil's arrest, people rolling me into rugs and dropping me out of windows." Her voice rose hysterically. "Are those two men *dead?*"

"Yes," Tsanko said curtly, standing up, "and there is no time to bury them, we will have to use a little dynamite and bury the cellar instead. Kosta . . ." He turned and spoke to the young man in Bulgarian. Kosta nodded and climbed out of the cellar.

Debby said accusingly, "This man knows your name, I heard him!"

"Yes," said Mrs. Pollifax gently, "I came to Bulgaria to meet him. I do hope you're not going to have hysterics, because we're still in great danger."

Debby stared at her and suddenly quieted. "No, I won't have hysterics. *Why* did you come to Bulgaria to meet him, Mrs. Pollifax?"

"Later," she told her.

They climbed together out of the crumbling cellar, bushes tearing at their faces, and after several minutes Tsanko followed and gestured them toward a hill some distance away. Here they waited in silence. Presently Kosta joined them, as well as a second young man, and as they walked over and down the hill Mrs. Pollifax heard the sound of a small, muffled explosion behind them, like very faint thunder.

Mr. Carleton Bemish had just been buried. *Requiescat in pace*, thought Mrs. Pollifax sadly.

13

"We are nearly there," said Tsanko.

Ahead of them stood a wall silhouetted against the moonlit sky, a solitary, abandoned wall holding back a hill grown over with grass. "We go inside this hill," he explained. "It hides a secret tunnel that once led to the fortress."

Kosta leaned over, pulling aside bushes to reveal a gap in the huge stones along the base of the wall. One by one they crawled into a narrow earthen tunnel, made an abrupt turn and emerged into a cave. Mrs. Pollifax heard Tsanko striking matches and suddenly light flared from a lantern. They were in a large room laced with roots, its ceiling braced by ancient timbers.

"You have given us much trouble, Amerikanski," Tsanko said, blowing out his match and turning up the wick of the lantern. Shaggy white brows completely shadowed his eyes. He looked tough, shrewd and weathered. Studying her face with equal frankness, he said, "Please —sit down, you are exhausted." From a corner he brought her a three-legged stool. From his pocket he removed a small vial, uncapped it and, leaning over the lantern, held it under her nose. "Smelling salts," he explained. "No, please—you look very faint."

"It's been a long day," confessed Mrs. Pollifax.

He carried the vial to Debby, the sharp smell of ammonia lingering behind him. He said dryly, "I believe this. I have observed you once in Sofia from a car. At that time the color of your face was surely five times brighter than at this minute." He sat across from her and said bluntly, "On that occasion in Sofia I thought you a foolish American lady. Now I am not so sure. Do you know you have been followed by the secret police since the night you arrived in Sofia? We have had severe doubts about you."

"I'm sorry," she said, nodding. "That's why you wanted to get me out of Sofia—I understand that now."

"Not for *your* safety," he pointed out harshly. "For ours. We began to fear that Shipkov had betrayed us."

"Oh no, Shipkov reached New York safely, thanks to you," she said warmly. "Are you the man who warned him on the street?"

Tsanko shook his head. "That was Boris."

"You have a marked talent for saving lives," she said gratefully.

He was watching her intently; now he shook his head. "You still have no idea of the danger you have been in, Amerikanski—from us—especially after you came to Tarnovo with two men still following you. I can assure you it was only the utmost good luck—for you!—that I hear you speak with the two men on the road, and hear this young lady scream. Until then I am sure you are friends with these men, and arranging big trap for me."

"But I thought I was the one walking into a trap," she told him in surprise.

He lifted his shoulders in a large and eloquent shrug. "Touché. But we begin to see that you are in trouble,

Amerikanski, you have blundered into something we know nothing about. How is this?"

"Philip Trenda," said Mrs. Pollifax. "Does that name mean anything to you?"

"It might," he said evasively and turned to Kosta, who had dropped in a corner with both hands across his eyes. "What is it?" he asked sharply, and then broke into Bulgarian.

"Is he all right?"

"He has never killed a man before," Tsanko explained. "He will feel better soon."

"You didn't answer my question about Philip Trenda, you know."

He shrugged. "One does not like to confess one listens to Radio Skolje, it is forbidden in my country. Yes, his arrest has caused a great noise in the Western world. But does this explain your being followed in Sofia by"— he removed a piece of paper from his pocket and read from it—"by one Mincho Kolarov, also one Assen Radev—"

"Two?" said Mrs. Pollifax blankly.

"And now these men."

"I don't understand," she said, puzzled. "I noticed a short gray-haired man in a gray suit—"

"That was Mincho Kolarov of the secret police. The other party, Assen Radev, we know nothing about. Late last night he returned to a collective farm outside of Sofia. He appears to raise geese."

"Geese!" echoed Mrs. Pollifax in astonishment.

"Yes. And now we have this Bemish, in company with a man never before seen by us."

"He's a man I've never seen before, either. Back in the cellar you said he was from the secret police. How could you know?"

"You saw me remove the wallet from his body. His papers carry the name of Titko Yugov, and this particular kind of identity card is carried only by members of our secret police."

He handed her the narrow card of plastic and she gave a start. *"It looks like a lottery ticket or a swimming pass,"* she heard herself say aloud, and she began to dig into her purse, dumping papers out all around her. "Here it is," she said in amazement. "I'd completely forgotten. What does this say? You see, it's exactly the same kind of card except it carries a different name. I've had it in my purse since Belgrade."

Tsanko took it, glanced it over and looked at her questioningly. He said quietly, "This one identifies its bearer as one Nikolai F. Dzhagarov, serial number 3891F in the Secret Security Police of the People's Republic of Bulgaria."

Debby, who had been leaning wearily against the wall, suddenly straightened. "That's *Nikki!*"

"Nikki," repeated Mrs. Pollifax. "So there it is—the proof. Nikki's not only Bulgarian, but he's a member of your police." The knowledge saddened her because it removed all hope that Philip's arrest had been an accident. "I think I'd better tell you the whole story," she said to Tsanko. "If I begin at the beginning, leaving out nothing, perhaps you can tell us what we've fallen into."

"I beg that you explain," Tsanko said with some relief.

Mrs. Pollifax began to talk, her glance occasionally falling upon Debby, whose face grew more and more incredulous. When she had finished it was Debby who broke the silence. "But you're one of those nasty CIA spies!" she wailed. "And those brakes were fixed to *kill* us? And our coming to Bulgaria was all part of a *plot?*"

"It is no wonder you needed smelling salts," Tsanko said, regarding Mrs. Pollifax with curiosity. "It becomes very simple upon hearing this. You know too much. In Bulgaria it is not wise to know too much, especially about something in which the secret police are involved."

"But what do I know?" protested Mrs. Pollifax.

"Let us consider—perhaps you are too near to see it. Certainly the luxuries in Bemish's apartment suggest a liberal reward for something, and Bemish himself has spoken of months of planning."

"Yes," said Mrs. Pollifax, nodding vigorously.

"This paper the Trenda boy gave to you in the air terminal"—he tapped it with a finger—"it would explain the trouble Nikki had at the border. Without it he could no longer prove he was secret police and his special privileges are denied him at Customs."

"All right," agreed Mrs. Pollifax.

"Your visit to Mr. Eastlake would have been observed, too—the walls of an Embassy are all ears. Tell me again what Bemish spoke to you in those last minutes in the cellar. He was about to kill you, and he was opening up. He believed he was explaining everything, even if it made no sense."

Mrs. Pollifax frowned, remembering. "He was very angry, very bitter," she said. "It was something about Stella having a brother, Petrov, who emigrated to America and made millions, but if he'd stayed in Bulgaria he would have had to share his money."

"Presumably with Bemish," said Tsanko with a quick smile.

"Yes. I asked him who Stella was, and he explained she was his wife. They received only 'hand-outs,' as he put it . . ." She stopped because Tsanko looked so startled.

"But there begins something," he said in surprise. "Bemish married a Bulgarian, you know. It is the habit here that when a woman marries a foreigner she is still identified—referred to—by her Bulgarian name. In Sofia, Mrs. Bemish is still known as Stella Trendafilov."

"Trendafilov!" repeated Mrs. Pollifax. "But that name sounds very much like—"

"Exactly," said Tsanko, nodding. "If a Trendafilov emigrated to America is it not possible he might shorten the name?"

"Good heavens," said Mrs. Pollifax.

Debby gasped, "But if you shorten Trendafilov it comes out Trenda! That would make Phil a relative—a nephew!"

"Well, well," murmured Mrs. Pollifax.

"But why would Mr. Bemish want to see his nephew in jail for espionage? I don't get it," Debby said helplessly.

"It is not necessary we 'get it,'" Tsanko told her firmly. "To draw conclusions so quickly would be very foolish. We must collect facts. To put them together must come later."

Mrs. Pollifax said dryly, "It's a little difficult not to put them together now. We've discovered that Philip is probably the son of a man named Peter Trenda, who's president of Trenda-Arctic Oil Company. Presumably that makes him a man of some wealth. Bemish, over here, has a rich brother-in-law in America named Petrov Trendafilov, and Bemish appears to have been quite involved in Philip's arrest. Perhaps it was even his idea."

"Wow, yes," said Debby eagerly.

"Do you think Mr. Bemish could have been a member of the secret police, like Nikki?"

Tsanko shook his head. "He would never be trusted. No, he is more likely an informer to the police—that is more his character and it would explain better his relationship with Nikki." He sighed. "There have always been bad rumors about Bemish, that he picks up money in strange ways, that he is cruel to his wife. She was very beautiful once, I am told. A pity."

Mrs. Pollifax said slowly, "Then it must begin with Bemish and Nikki—Philip's arrest, I mean. *That's* what Debby and I know that we shouldn't."

The lantern sputtered and the flame began streaming, its light unbelievably golden. Tsanko leaned over and adjusted the wick, dimming the light, and they became hollow-eyed ghosts again. "But it has become something much bigger now," he said with narrowed eyes. "Do not forget, Amerikanski, you have been under surveillance by genuine members of the secret police. How they became involved, and why . . ." Tsanko was thoughtful. "I smell something very rotten here, I experience deep curiosity. My inquiries must be very discreet, however, because of what happened tonight."

"But they're both dead, even buried," pointed out Debby.

Mrs. Pollifax looked at her. "There's Nikki still back in Sofia."

"Oh God, yes," she said, tears springing to her eyes. "You *will* find out something?" she asked Tsanko.

"Yes, we'll want to know," Mrs. Pollifax told him soberly.

"I keep trying to remember back in Yugoslavia," Debby said in an anguished voice. "Before all this happened. Phil never mentioned having relatives in Bulgaria, but he did act uptight about his reasons for not coming here with us. He just kept saying 'I can't go'—very firmly —but once he said his father would be furious if he went. Except he didn't say why."

Tsanko nodded. "His father was sensible. If he is Bulgarian and once fled the country there is always the fear of something. One never knows of what, but the Intelligence here is very excellent." He sighed. "However, all of this is conjecture, which I dislike. We must next verify."

Mrs. Pollifax was removing hatpins from her hat, which she now handed to him. "The passports are in the crown," she explained. "I'm told there are eight of them for you inside."

"Inside the *hat?*" he said in astonishment.

"Passports?" echoed Debby, wide-eyed. "So that's why you're meeting him!"

Tsanko turned the hat over with amusement. "We will be most interested to examine this construction. Ah,

American technology. We hear of it even here." He looked up as a second young man entered; his voice warmed as he greeted him. "This is Encho," he explained. "He has driven the black Renault back into Tarnovo and left it parked on the main street. If the car was seen coming in to Tsaravets then it has now been seen leaving as well. If you go back now"—he pulled out a heavy old-fashioned gold watch and glanced at it—"I think you must. Your absence will be noted."

"But the inquiries?" insisted Mrs. Pollifax. "You said you'd make inquiries. When will we hear what you learn about Philip?"

He looked surprised. "But you have given me the hat, which you tell me contains passports. Your job is complete, you can be out of Bulgaria by tomorrow noon."

She shook her head. "That's impossible, absolutely impossible."

"Why?"

She thought what a *lived* man he looked, square and shaggy, his lined face burned dark by sun and wind. "I don't like people trying to kill me," she said quietly. "I liked Philip Trenda and he's Debby's friend. He's very young, and I don't believe anyone else in Bulgaria—including, perhaps, the American Embassy—really cares."

"But you do?"

"Someone *must,*" she said fiercely.

"Then we will meet again," Tsanko told her, and he picked up the bird's nest hat and returned it to her. It was a gesture that completely took Mrs. Pollifax aback. He was handing her the passports—the lives of his friends—as a promise. "We will meet in the morning, I hope. If possible, Encho will come to the hotel for you. Encho lives here in Tarnovo, he drives a government taxi for tourists. He also speaks a little English.

"But now it is past midnight," he said, rising. "Balkantourist will be upset enough with your being in Tarnovo instead of Borovets, and two men have been killed tonight, wiped off the face of the earth. This is dangerous in any country. It will be a busy night for us."

Mrs. Pollifax held out the hat to him. "You've just given me back what I was assigned to deliver to you. Surely it's not professional for me to accept this?"

He smiled faintly and there was the hint of a twinkle in his eyes. "I am not sure either of us is professional, is this not possible?"

She looked at him in astonishment, and something like recognition arose between them.

"It is a long walk back," he said, escorting her to the cave's entrance. "When you have seen the Bulgarian mountains in moonlight you see my country at its best. Sleep well, Amerikanski," he added.

She nodded, and she and Debby followed Kosta from the cave.

14

At CIA headquarters in Langley Field, Virginia, it had been a trying Thursday. An ambassador had been abducted in South America the night before, and this morning an agent was missing in Hong Kong. There was also the continuing puzzle of young Philip Trenda, whose arrest was filling the front pages of the newspapers. Yesterday the State Department had asked Carstairs to see what he could discover about the situation through less conventional channels. It was a nuisance being called in on the job. Carstairs had already been summoned Upstairs twice for conferences and his routine work was piling up on the desk.

Having been involved in this crisis for only twenty-four hours Carstairs admitted to almost no progress and no new leads at all. He glanced now over a routine report on the affair from a B. Eastlake at the United States Embassy in Sofia. It was an abbreviated memo, a digest of the hour-by-hour reports coming from Sofia. Halfway down the first page Carstairs noticed a reference by Eastlake to two American tourists who had come to the Embassy on Tuesday. They had managed to suggest that Philip had been lured into Bulgaria by a young Yugoslavian traveling under a German passport.

There were always people to suggest this sort of thing and Carstairs noted that quite rightly Eastlake placed small faith in the story. He had given it only three lines in the report.

But Eastlake's job was judicial and diplomatic; Carstairs, on the other hand, lived and worked in a world of improbabilities, fantasies and the completely irrational. He pressed the buzzer for Bishop and handed him the report.

"Get me detailed information about these two tourists Eastlake talked to in Sofia. Exactly what was said, and why, and what sort of people they are. I want to know today."

"Right, sir," said Bishop, and went out.

Carstairs sighed. Nothing about Trenda's arrest made the slightest sense so far. The State Department couldn't figure out what the Bulgarians were up to, or what they planned to do. The Embassy in Sofia had still not been allowed to contact young Trenda. There were no details at all about the espionage charges, and none of this boded well for Philip. So far as Carstairs had been able to discover, the boy had no connection with political or subversive groups. He'd gone to public schools and then to the University of Illinois. He was the only child of a rich man. He wrote poetry, and the nearest he'd come to revolt against any system at all was a short article in his school paper on the current injustices of the draft. If he'd been engaged in suspicious activities they surely must have begun after he reached Europe in June. At this moment his being accused of espionage seemed utterly far-fetched, but of course it had to be checked out, and thoroughly.

Carstairs realized he felt desperately sorry for the boy. In only one area of his arrest had he been lucky: someone had caught the story at once, and it had captured the attention of newspapers all over Europe. This was an enormous help to him, although Carstairs knew how fickle such publicity could be, too. If Trenda wasn't freed soon—by the sheer weight of that publicity—a fresh crisis would move him off the front pages and the story would gradually die. He'd seen it happen. That would leave the State Department in charge, and sometimes the diplomatic exchanges went on ad infinitum. Three or four years from now Trenda might emerge from prison in Bulgaria and rate a small story on page two. Readers would say with a frown, "Familiar name, Trenda . . . good God, has he been in prison all these *years?*"

Bishop knocked and walked in, his usually cheerful face clouded. "Something new from Sofia?" asked Carstairs.

"From Sofia, yes," said Bishop stiffly. "Nothing to do with the Trenda affair, however. It's the weekly *pâté de foie gras* report from Assen Radev. It's just been decoded."

Carstairs' glance sharpened. "Is Mrs. Pollifax all right? Did he switch the coats?"

Bishop only looked disapproving as he handed over the report.

He read: WHO IS THIS 10573 YOU SENT STOP ANY EXCHANGE OF COATS IMPOSSIBLE STOP REPEAT IMPOSSIBLE STOP EVEN BURGLARY FAILED STOP NEVER STAYS IN ONE PLACE STOP NOW GONE TO BOROVETS BUT ISN'T THERE STOP AM RETURNING TO WORK STOP WHY ARE SECRET POLICE TRAILING 10573 STOP.

When he had finished reading it Carstairs began to slowly, softly swear. When he ran out of expletives he added in an exhausted voice, "Those damn fools Upstairs. And Radev certainly has a neat way of planting bombshells, hasn't he? Why are the secret police trailing Mrs. Pollifax indeed!"

Bishop's face softened. "It could be Tsanko's men

trailing her, couldn't it? Radev may have misunderstood the situation."

"Do you really think so?" asked Carstairs bitterly.

Bishop shook his head.

When he'd gone Carstairs lit a cigarette and considered this new complication. It wasn't only the reference to secret police that troubled him, he didn't like the sound of Mrs. Pollifax going off to Borovets and not arriving there. Had she been arrested? And why Borovets? She had a car, it was true, but nothing had been said about her leaving Sofia. The tailor shop was in Sofia, and Tsanko was in Sofia. He didn't like it. Damn it, he thought, he'd told her to make a fast exit if anything looked suspicious. Why the hell hadn't she bolted?

He thought furiously, She trusts too many people.

He'd told Bishop this wasn't Sears Roebuck and it wasn't Gimbels they worked for, but he knew that he'd meant it for himself. He loathed worrying like this about one of his people. He considered putting through a transatlantic call to the Hotel Rila to check on her, and then he discarded the idea as idiotic. His call would be monitored. Even if he reached Mrs. Pollifax he couldn't possibly say, "Get rid of the coat you're wearing–burn it, hide it, cut it up, give it to somebody." She wouldn't have the slightest idea what he meant–it was the hat she'd been assigned to protect, not her coat–and the people monitoring his call would have only *too* clear an idea of what he meant.

Damn, he thought, and as Bishop walked in again he snapped, "Well?"

There was a twinkle in Bishop's eye. What was more alarming, he'd brought Carstairs a cup of steaming hot coffee. Bishop never volunteered coffee unless it was for purposes of fortification during a difficult moment.

Almost cheerfully Bishop said, "The State Department has been in touch with Eastlake at the U. S. Embassy in Sofia, sir. You remember you asked for details on the two tourists who suggested Trenda might have been deliberately brought into Bulgaria?"

"Of course," Carstairs said.

"Here's the report. You might like to take a look at the names of those tourists first–they're at the bottom of the page. Names and passport numbers."

Carstairs grasped the paper and allowed his glance to drop to the bottom. He read: Mrs. Virgil Pollifax, Apt. 4-B, Hemlock Arms, New Brunswick, N.J., U.S.A.

He exploded. "What the hell! Bishop," he demanded furiously, "can you tell me what the devil Mrs. Pollifax is doing mixing into something that's none of her business? Doesn't she realize she has eight passports in her hat, not to mention that blasted coat Radev's been incapable of switching?"

"She doesn't know about the coat, sir," Bishop reminded him silkily.

"But doesn't she realize she's not in New Brunswick, New Jersey? Doesn't she understand she's not supposed to *meddle*? Bishop, what the hell are you grinning about?"

"You, sir. Mrs. Pollifax is so much like you."

"What?" snapped Carstairs.

Bishop nodded. "She goes off on tangents. Operates on impulse and trusts her intuition. When she stops upsetting you, sir, it'll be because she's turned into a well-behaved, well-trained and completely predictable operator. You'll sleep nights and stop swearing. And then she'll be like all your professional agents, and of no use to you at all, will she?"

Carstairs glared at him. "Are you suggesting I run this department on nothing but impulse and intuition, Bishop?"

"I have never known you to follow the book, sir," said Bishop serenely. "That's why you're so successful isn't it? Incidentally, your telephone's buzzing, sir."

Angrily, Carstairs flipped switches and barked into the receiver. He listened and his expression changed. Hanging up he said, "Something's happening. The Bulgarian Embassy's going to make an important announcement in ten minutes."

15

Mrs. Pollifax was awakened at nine o'clock the next morning in Tarnovo by an urgent hammering on the door and a message—acted out in pantomine—that she was wanted at once on the telephone in the lobby. Mrs. Pollifax threw her coat over her pajamas and hurried downstairs.

She had expected it to be Nevena, and braced herself. But it was not Nevena, it was the American Embassy in Sofia, and after being told to wait she at last heard the faint but unmistakable voice of Mr. Eastlake.

"However did you find me!" she exclaimed.

Eastlake's voice sounded tired. "With difficulty. Have you heard from Balkantourist this morning?"

"No."

"You will," he said dryly. "They told me where you are. They seem rather angry, though. There was some kind of accident?"

"Among other things," she said. He couldn't have called about the accident and she told him so.

"Quite true," he said. "I recall your concern about

young Trenda, and knowing that you're still in the country I thought you might enjoy your vacation more if you knew he's being released this afternoon. At two o'clock, at the Embassy."

"Released?" echoed Mrs. Pollifax incredulously.

"Released. You sound surprised."

"Surprised but delighted," she said hastily. She wondered how she could possibly explain her intense surprise, when Philip's confinement had brought three attempts on her life, the latest of them last night. "At two o'clock, you said?"

"Yes. If you have that young Debby's address you might like to reassure her as well, although she's bound to be reading it in the major western Europe newspapers."

"Yes," said Mrs. Pollifax, and then, "What made them . . . that is . . ."

"Diplomatic pressure, I imagine," Eastlake said crisply. "I suspect the Kremlin intervened as well. Because of Bemish's early dispatches the news has been headlined since Tuesday morning in London, Paris, New York, Oslo. . . . But all's well that ends well, eh, Mrs. Pollifax? Happy journeying."

"Yes . . . and thank you so much," she said, hanging up and hurried upstairs to tell Debby. "Philip's being released at two this afternoon in Sofia."

Debby sat bolt upright. "Great!" she shouted and rolled to her feet in that same beautifully fluid athletic manner that had so dazzled Mrs. Pollifax on the night of the burglary.

"Breakfast first, and then packing," said Mrs. Pollifax hurriedly, but even so she was summoned to her second telephone call while still in bare feet.

This time it was Nevena, a very excited and aggrieved Nevena, who wanted to know what Mrs. Pollifax was doing in Tarnovo when she was supposed to be in Borovets.

"Well," said Mrs. Pollifax, drawing a deep breath, "I met some people who told me Tarnovo was too beautiful to be missed. I met them only a block from the hotel when I took a wrong turning—"

"How could you take a wrong turning?" demanded Nevena. "The directions were plain, very clear. I saw them. They said—"

"I took this wrong turning," continued Mrs. Pollifax blandly, "and I met these people."

"What people?"

"English, I think, or Canadian. The man was quite tall and had a scar. On his left cheek," she added artistically. "And I decided to go to Tarnovo instead."

She could almost hear Nevena's foot stamping. "You Americans," she said indignantly. "You see what happens now, your car is wrecked. They wake me up to say it will take very long to fix the car and you will need a new car in Tarnovo when all the time you are supposed to be in Borovets. First you come to Sofia and are to stay, and then you meet some people who tell you Sofia is not the real Bulgaria—"

She has an excellent memory, thought Mrs. Pollifax.

"And now you meet some other peoples—"

"I'm truly sorry," said Mrs. Pollifax, wearying of the joke. "In America, you see, we're quite free to—"

She had made her point; Nevena interrupted, but her voice was reproachful now rather than angry. "It is very difficult for me when you change the itinerary. How can I give you the idyllic service when you jump so? There will be another car for you at 1 P.M., leaving Sofia soon to reach you, and the driver will personally return you to the Hotel Rila."

"I'd rather leave earlier," said Mrs. Pollifax. "I could take the train?"

"There will be the car," Nevena said flatly, and then as a dutiful afterthought she added, "You are not hurt by the accident, Mrs. Pollifax?"

"I was not hurt," said Mrs. Pollifax and hung up. She

had just seen Encho enter the lobby, catch sight of her and quietly jerk his head toward the street.

She and Debby sat primly upright in the rear seat of Encho's battered and dusty taxi. Encho said in his broken English that Tsanko had news for them, and Mrs. Pollifax had said, "Yes, and I have news for him, too." But it was necessary for Encho to drive them first through Tarnovo, slowing and pointing at houses of historical distinction to establish the fact that they were tourists in case they were being watched. At last he stopped in front of a small wooden house that clung to the side of a hill. "My house," he said proudly. "Tsanko waits." When Debby started to climb out, too, he gestured her back. "Tsanko say you take pictures," he said and handed her a camera. "To explain the stop."

Inside the house Tsanko was pacing up and down the dark, slant-floored living room, and at sight of the expression on his face Mrs. Pollifax was jolted. She had expected this to be a happy meeting, and although it was true that he must have gone without sleep and done a great deal of work since they'd seen him, she was not prepared for such a grim, drawn face. "Something is the matter?" she said breathlessly.

His voice was harsh. "I have made the inquiries about your young American and it is not good."

She stared at him in disbelief. "Not good! But I've just heard—whatever do you mean?"

"They have all gone mad, insane. I cannot foresee how he comes out of this alive."

"But he must, he's going to!" gasped Mrs. Pollifax.

Tsanko ceased his pacing and turned to her. "I beg your pardon—sit down," he said. "Please." But he did not sit down, he resumed his restless pacing instead. "It is like this—please listen carefully. My government was taken completely by surprise with this Trenda's arrest. Madness!" he said in an aside, both hands to his head.

"The government knew nothing! It was confronted with the *fait accompli.*"

"Well, then," said Mrs. Pollifax hopefully.

He savagely interrupted her. "In Bulgaria such matters lead to blood baths, Amerikanski. You are a government—think a moment—and you discover this situation has brought the world down on your head. It makes grave conditions internationally, this arrest of an American student. Headlines. Protests. *And you knew nothing about it.* This is embarrassing, you understand?"

"Very," she said, nodding.

"As the government, you cannot afford to say you know nothing, it loses the face, it implies no power. But you cannot publicly sanction it, either. You are stuck. You must find a way out, eh?"

"Yes, and—"

His hand cut the air. "Heads have rolled. The chief of the security police has been taken mysteriously ill and has resigned. He has been replaced by General Ignatov."

"General Ignatov!"

He halted, peering at her from under his thick brows. "You know this name?"

"I was asked to question you about him if possible. We came to Sofia on the same plane, too—there was an unscheduled stop in Rumania to pick him up."

"Well, I can tell you now that he has just become head of our secret security." He shook his head. "I fear for my country. He is in charge personally of this mess, and he has announced suddenly to the foreign press that at two o'clock this afternoon Philip Trenda will be released and flown out of the country to Belgrade."

Mrs. Pollifax nodded happily. "Yes, isn't that wonderful? Mr. Eastlake phoned me about it, it was so terribly kind of him."

Tsanko said grimly, "I do not believe it. Something will

intervene—a last minute cancellation, a delay—because the ransom has not yet been paid."

"The *what?*" gasped Mrs. Pollifax.

Tsanko nodded, his eyes narrowed. "Money. A million dollars in hard currency from the Trenda fortune. Money in American dollars."

"A million!" whispered Mrs. Pollifax.

"Yes. To be paid by Philip Trenda's father personally into a Swiss bank in Zurich on Monday morning at ten o'clock."

"But this is only Thursday, and if Philip is freed to-day—"

"Exactly. Why would he pay this great ransom if his son is safe?"

Mrs. Pollifax stared at him, appalled. "You think this announcement is a fraud? Something made up by General Ignatov to placate the press, to stall until Monday?"

Tsanko abruptly sat down and looked into her face. "I will be frank with you, Amerikanski. I am deeply disturbed over this General Ignatov's involvement in the matter. There are details to this situation I do not like. Always it is interesting to me to see who swims to the top at such a time. I find most interesting that it is General Ignatov who offers instant solutions to my government in this crisis."

She understood at once. "Does he know Nikki?" she asked.

"You are very quick," he acknowledged with a smile. "Yes, it happens that he does. My informant tells me General Ignatov knows quite a number of young members of the secret police. Is this not a surprising coincidence?"

Mrs. Pollifax said slowly, "Carleton Bemish knew Nikki, and Nikki—"

"Is a protégé of General Ignatov," finished Tsanko for her.

"They were both on the same plane with me—at least

from Rumania to Sofia," said Mrs. Pollifax. "There was no point of contact, though."

"Yet this Nikki was allowed a passport to leave Bulgaria and go to Yugoslavia to bring back young Trenda. He could have managed this only with powerful backing," pointed out Tsanko. "This I have found astonishing from the start. Please note as well that although my government knew nothing of this plot there were bona fide members of the secret police keeping you under surveillance. Someone with influence is behind all this."

"You think it's General Ignatov," she said, nodding.

Tsanko said dryly, "I always think. The coincidences begin to grow surprising."

"There's more?"

He nodded. "The arrests began at once last night. Included among them are some members of secret security. Our friend Nikki, however, was given promotion at once."

Mrs. Pollifax's lips formed an O out of comprehension.

"Out of hundreds of secret police it is Nikki that is singled out. The arrests are of much interest as well. Each person arrested has been severe critic of General Ignatov, or is out-and-out enemy, and several are men to whom he owes much money. Creditors, in a word."

"He's planning to overthrow the government," said Mrs. Pollifax flatly.

Tsanko nodded. "I think so. Not immediately, but soon —and my government is too blind at this moment, too upset to see. All that General Ignatov has needed is to have the secret police in his pocket. And last night he was given this like a gift."

"Oh dear," said Mrs. Pollifax.

"My informant is among his enemies," he added sadly. "He, too, is member of the secret police, an old friend. He fears now for his life."

"I'm sorry," she said. "He's one of your group?"

Tsanko shook his head. "No, but he has given us much valued information. It is he who told us the man Shipkov was to be arrested." He smiled wryly. "He and Shipkov shared an interest in General Ignatov, they nearly met one night watching General Ignatov's home. Each one occupied—I am told—a different flowerbed."

Mrs. Pollifax smiled. "That must have been funny. But Tsanko, why the ransom? If General Ignatov now has what he wanted from the beginning—"

"Why not?" said Tsanko with a shrug. "Doubtless he will use the ransom as evidence against his enemies. He will say, 'Look at the plot—all this for Western currency!' Each dollar will be a nail in their coffins. He can impound the money and present it to his government—that will earn him another medal. And there is nothing like a million in American dollars to make oneself popular." He shook his head sadly. "Poor Bemish. He wanted only a little money for wine and women and cigarettes, and see how he has been used by these two."

"And Philip?" she asked quietly.

He nodded. "Exactly. That is why I beseech Encho to take you to Sofia at once, in his taxi—you can pay him a little something for it?—so that you can be at the Embassy at two. Myself, I must go back also, but alone."

"Balkantourist is sending . . ." Mrs. Pollifax stopped and shook her head. "We'll go with Encho," she said. "I'm very alarmed about this." Removing her bird's nest hat, again she gave it to him. "Please—these are the passports I was sent to give you."

He nodded. "I will accept them now, although—alas—three of the people these would have rescued were taken to Panchevsky Institute last night. At General Ignatov's orders."

"Taken where?" she asked.

"That is the name of a mental institute in Sofia, now filled with political prisoners—who may be the sanest of us all," he added with a sigh.

She said swiftly, "You doubt your government."

"I would protect my government against General Ignatov with my *life*." His fierceness startled her.

Forgetting discretion, she asked bluntly, "Tsanko, who are you? All this information, and you've collected it in hours. And Tarnovo," she persisted. "You're free to travel here without question?"

He laughed. "I have a summer home here in the hills, which is why I come to Tarnovo. As to who I am—I'm a good communist, a patriot and also—God help me—a humanist."

"But are you against the Russians?"

His brows shot up. "Please—not at all! They protect us from the wolves, they give us years of peace, some prosperity." He hesitated and then he said soberly, "But before I die I would like to see my country move, have direction. We go nowhere in Bulgaria, and our young people deserve better. They grow bitter, despondent, strangled by bureaucracy—"

"You're a nationalist!" she cried triumphantly.

He laughed. "Please—such words are very dangerous. It is best we not talk political, Amerikanski. Allow me the pleasure to enjoy my first American, like a good wine, eh?"

On the ride back to Sofia, Debby said suddenly, "I don't *want* to like you, Mrs. Pollifax, and I shall keep trying not to like you, but I do want you to know that I'm grateful to be alive today."

"I confess to a certain pleasure in it myself," said Mrs. Pollifax, startled.

Debby said, "My parents give me everything." She said it as though she were reciting something too important to be given significance. "They say they want me to have everything because they had such a hard time when they were young. But when I ask for something *I* want they tell me I'm spoiled and ungrateful. My mother always wants me to confide in her," she said. "Girl stuff. The one time I did tell her something important she was shocked and called my father and they punished me. My father spends all his time making money and my mother spends all her time spending it, shopping with her friends or playing bridge. They're bored and miserable and they want me to grow up to be just like them. And I can't—I won't, I won't, I *won't*."

A boil is being lanced, thought Mrs. Pollifax, and said without expression, "I see."

"Phil's parents are different. I think it's why I like him so much. Do you know he had to earn every cent he's spending on this trip to Europe?" Her voice was awed.

Mrs. Pollifax glanced at her with interest.

"Of course you can now start explaining my parents," Debby pointed out. "Don't you want to?"

"Not at all," said Mrs. Pollifax truthfully.

"You're not going to tell me they mean well?"

"I don't know whether they mean well or not," said Mrs. Pollifax tartly. "I've never met them."

"Don't you even want to give advice?"

Mrs. Pollifax laughed. "No, because you'll work it out for yourself. You strike me as being a very intelligent young person. And also," she added thoughtfully, "because you came very, *very* near to losing your life last night."

"What's that have to do with it?" asked Debby indignantly.

"Everything, I think," said Mrs. Pollifax musingly. "It's the greatest revolution of all. But not recommended in large doses," she added firmly, "and now we must keep it from ever happening again."

They were late in reaching Sofia, and there was no time to go first to the hotel and leave their suitcases. It was already five minutes past the hour when Encho deposited them at the Embassy; they had time only to wave good-bye to him as they flew across the pavement. Now it was Debby who was in command as she went to the desk and asked if Philip Trenda was really being released today.

"The group is in the library," said the clerk stiffly.

"Group?"

"Mr. Trenda is meeting with foreign reporters."

"Then he's really *here?*" cried Debby excitedly.

"But of course," said the clerk, looking at them in surprise.

A feeling of deep relief filled Mrs. Pollifax: miracles did happen, and Tsanko had been wrong.

"Wonderful," Debby cried. "Oh, Mrs. Pollifax, isn't this a beautiful, beautiful day? He's here, he's free, he's *out*. Where's the library?"

The clerk patiently ushered them down the hall and into the library. It was a large sunny room, half filled with people and cameras. Unfortunately the twenty or thirty men present—as well as cameras—were all in one corner of the room, forming a tight, almost inviolate circle around two people who stood against the wall.

"We really are late," murmured Mrs. Pollifax, standing on tiptoe.

"Oh blast, I can't see him," Debby said, jumping up and down.

Mrs. Pollifax looked about for a chair, found one and stood on it. "I can see his head," she told Debby, peering between and over the newsmen. "He's grown a small beard. Try a chair, Debby. There, do you see him?"

"I can't—yes! There he is."

Phil stood next to Eastlake, his shoulders slouched; he was wearing dark glasses against the popping of the flashbulbs. He looked thinner, weary, lacking in animation. I wonder if he was drugged while in prison, thought Mrs. Pollifax.

"Please, gentlemen," Eastlake was saying, "he has a plane to catch, and we've very little time. But as you can see, he's been released and that's the important thing. Keep your questions very brief, please."

"Were you treated well?" called someone from the rear row.

Philip replied in a low husky voice.

"We can't hear him back here," called out a man with a British accent.

"He said he was treated well and is looking forward to getting home now," Eastlake said. "He has a slight cold, touch of laryngitis."

"Is he aware that his arrest made sensational headlines all over the world?"

Eastlake answered for him, smiling. "I don't think he realizes anything, he's been completely out of touch and we've had little time to talk."

"Does he hold it against the Bulgarian government that he was arrested like this?"

Eastlake looked pained. "Gentlemen, please, I refer you to the written statement which has been distributed among you all. He says he holds no personal animosity toward the Bulgarian government, he's only glad to be free and going home. And now I think we really must leave for the airport. If you will excuse us, gentlemen . . ."

There was a fresh storm of flashbulbs and then a path was made for Eastlake and Philip. They passed very near to Mrs. Pollifax, who stood back. Debby, on the other hand, moved forward. "Phil?" she said as he passed by.

His head turned slightly—Mrs. Pollifax could no longer see his face—and then he followed Eastlake out of the room and down the hall. The newsmen pressed forward, separating Mrs. Pollifax from Debby.

In a matter of seconds the room had emptied and Mrs. Pollifax turned to see Debby leaning against the nearest wall, her eyes closed and both of her hands pressed to her stomach. She looked as if she were about to be very ill.

"Debby?" faltered Mrs. Pollifax.

Through clenched teeth Debby said, "It wasn't Phil. Do you understand—*that wasn't Phil.*"

Mrs. Pollifax stared at her. "Wasn't Phil," she echoed,

and suddenly sat down because she realized at once that Debby was right: there had been no sense of recognition, of familiarity when she'd glimpsed him. The height and build and general characteristics were the same, but it was someone else—an imposter—with laryngitis to disguise the voice, a stubble of beard to confuse the jawline and dark glasses to conceal the eyes.

Tsanko had said that there would be a last-minute cancellation, some kind of delay—but this was worse, this was far more ominous because in the eyes of the world it had been Philip Trenda who had just walked out with Eastlake, and that meant . . .

"Oh God," Debby said, covering her face with her hands. "Phil's still in prison—and *nobody knows?*"

Mrs. Pollifax nodded.

Debby uncovered her face and looked at Mrs. Pollifax. "I'm scared," she said. "I've never been so scared in my life."

"It's better to be angry," said Mrs. Pollifax thoughtfully. "This is why they tried to kill us last night—*they* knew."

"But how can they get away with it? There'll be Phil's parents . . ."

Mrs. Pollifax said sadly, "I don't think we have to speculate—I'm sure they'll have thought of everything." But what that *everything* might be was too chilling for her to name yet. "I wish you'd screamed in front of everyone as soon as you saw it wasn't Philip," she added forlornly.

"I couldn't," Debby said. "I'm inhibited. I am. I really am. All those people, and then I wasn't absolutely sure until they were walking out." She shivered.

"Well, we've certainly got to tell Mr. Eastlake as soon as he returns from the airport."

Debby shook her head. "You can, but not me. He'd only insist that I leave the country again."

"But you just said you were frightened."

"For Phil, not for myself. Actually I'm terrified for him if you want the truth."

Mrs. Pollifax believed her. How oddly quixotic the child was! Filled with prickly hostilities and impulsive bursts of warmth, deeply troubled and only half formed but unquestioningly generous. "I'll see Mr. Eastlake alone," she said, and then reconsidered. She could hear herself explaining all that she knew to Eastlake and she could hear his protestations. "My dear Mrs. Pollifax, what an outrageous story you tell! Can you substantiate just one of these wild accusations?"

And she couldn't. She couldn't produce Tsanko, and she couldn't reveal her own role in this or even prove what lay behind the series of accidents. Was there anything she *could* prove? Yes, there was.

"Dry your eyes, Debby," she said, and stood up. "I've an idea—let's go."

"Go where?"

"To see Mrs. Bemish before she learns she's a widow."

Debby's reaction was forthright: "Ech," she said distastefully.

The smell of cooked cabbage competed today with the odor of a very strong antiseptic. Mrs. Pollifax reached the third landing of the apartment house with Debby close behind her, and knocked on the door of 301. She wondered if she was drawn here by guilt, because if she had not interfered with Bemish's greedy plans he would still be alive. Even more pertinent, however, she felt a need to share this crisis with someone who might care about Philip. Carstairs would be appalled at her coming here, and Tsanko might be shocked, but it was time to prove beyond doubt that a relationship existed between the Bemishes in Sofia and the Trendas in America.

The door opened a few inches to frame a stoic, browned face. "Mrs. Bemish?"

"*Da.*" The door opened wider and Mrs. Pollifax recognized the drab little woman she had glimpsed on her earlier visit. This was a peasant's face, shuttered, proud, seamed and crisscrossed with lines. On the left cheekbone a bruise was turning purple; Bemish's legacy, no doubt. What an odious man!

She said, "Do you speak English? May we come in and talk to you?"

The door opened wider and Mrs. Pollifax and Debby entered the dreary, cluttered apartment. "I speak small English," the woman admitted. "But—my husband not here. He left with business and is not back yet."

"I know he's not here," said Mrs. Pollifax. "We came to see *you*."

"Yes?" The woman had sat down opposite them in a chair, her hands slack in her lap. Now she looked startled and uneasy.

"We came to ask about your brother in America."

"Petrov! Oh yes, yes," she said eagerly, nodding her head.

"You do have a brother in America, then," said Mrs. Pollifax, exchanging a quick glance with Debby.

"Da," the woman cried excitedly, and jumped to her feet and hurried into the next room. When she returned she carried pictures with her. "Petrov," she said proudly. "Very good man. He is called Peter now."

"Peter Trenda?" asked Mrs. Pollifax.

"Here's *Phil!"* cried Debby, leaning over the pictures. "See?"

"You know Philip?" said Mrs. Bemish in an astonished voice. "You know Petrov's son?"

"We're friends," Debby told her, nodding.

"You and Philip!" The woman's eyes fed hungrily on Debby's face. "This is much honor," she whispered.

Leaning forward, Mrs. Pollifax said, "And do you know that Petrov's son—your nephew—is here in Sofia?"

The woman drew in her breath harshly. *"Here? Bora,* how is this?"

"He's in Sofia in jail. In prison."

Mrs. Bemish looked bewildered. "Why should Petrov's son be in prison?"

"Dzhagarov and your husband arranged this."

"Dzhagarov and–" She bit off her words abruptly, looking frightened and angry. "I do not believe this."

"Do you know the word 'ransom'? They want a great deal of money from your brother Petrov. You must know your nephew was visiting Yugoslavia?"

"*Da*," the woman said. "His first trip to Europe. Yugoslavia."

"Nikki was there, too, and persuaded him to come here to Bulgaria."

The woman looked from one face to another, studying each of them. "Philip never come to Bulgaria," she said, shaking her head. "Never. Not good."

"But he did come," Debby told her. "I think Nikki drugged him to get him here. And he was arrested at once here in Sofia–I was with him when it happened. He was charged with espionage."

"What is this word 'espionage'?"

"Spying," said Mrs. Pollifax.

Mrs. Bemish said sharply, "I cannot believe. There are no Americans at Panchevsky Institute. You lie."

"Where?"

"Panchevsky Institute. I work there," said Mrs. Bemish. "I know. Every night I work there, eight o'clock to six in morning. I work there in kitchens. No Americans." She shook her head fiercely.

"You mean the prison here is called that," Mrs. Pollifax said, remembering Tsanko's words. "But working in the kitchens, would you *know?*" She leaned forward. "They say it's in newspapers all over Europe that Philip Trenda has been arrested on charges of espionage. Your husband sent out the early news stories, but it's not in the papers here because–" She stopped.

Something she said had triggered a response. Mrs.

Bemish looked suddenly chilled and old. "When?" she whispered.

"Monday," Debby told her.

They waited while the woman wrestled with some fact or piece of gossip overheard or guessed; it must have been this because her refusal to believe had been replaced by doubt. She was silent a long time and then her eyes narrowed and she stood up and walked over to the window, pulling back the curtains and stood there staring out. "So," she said at last and turned, her eyes hard. "So."

Mrs. Pollifax saw that she was trembling, and then, as she watched, Mrs. Bemish threw back her head and with her lips shut tight in a grimace there came from her throat a harsh animal cry of pain. It was terrible. In her cry was expressed all the anguish and the humiliation of years, suffered stoically and in private. It was indecent to watch, and Mrs. Pollifax looked away.

After several minutes, regaining control, Mrs. Bemish said in a lifeless voice, "At Panchevsky Institute—high up—there is special room for ШПИОН. Spies," she explained. "On Monday they say young boy—very young —is brought in. He is foreigner. The guards say how young he is, with much black hair, very Bulgarian but speaking no Bulgarian." She looked pleadingly at Mrs. Pollifax. "If this is Philip . . ."

"Can you find out? Could you at least find out what language he does speak? Or what he's done?"

The woman looked frightened. "I *try*," she said, and then, "My husband kill me if he find out."

Debby started to speak, but Mrs. Pollifax shook her head. "You may have to choose," she said. "You may have to choose between your husband and your nephew." It did not feel the right moment to tell her that her husband was dead.

"For Petrov I do this," said Mrs. Bemish simply. "He is good brother, always. He write letters. Every month he send two hundred *leva* to help us." She lifted her eyes to Mrs. Pollifax and said fiercely, "For Petrov I would die."

Somewhat taken aback by her passion, Mrs. Pollifax nodded; she believed her. Rising she said, "We'd better leave now, but we'll see you again, Mrs. Bemish. Tomorrow, I think. Friday."

Mrs. Bemish only nodded.

They tiptoed out of the apartment, quietly closing the door behind them. "That poor woman," Debby said in a hushed voice.

But a startling idea had just occurred to Mrs. Pollifax and she was turning it over speculatively in her mind. Its simplicity dazzled her. As they reached the ground floor she asked of herself, "Why not?"

"Why not what?" said Debby. "Mrs. Pollifax, you're looking spooky again."

"It's so tempting," confided Mrs. Pollifax thoughtfully. "We have an Underground, and a woman who would die for her brother . . ." Caution intruded and she shook her head. "No, no, impossible." But caution held no appeal. "Let's make another call," she suggested, and felt suddenly rejuvenated.

16

Number nine Vasil Levski had already locked its doors, but a solitary woman remained working under a strong light behind the counter. Mrs. Pollifax knocked and then rattled the door. "Is the man who speaks English here?" she asked when the woman opened the door.

"Englis?" The woman shrugged and went to the rear and shouted.

Presently Mrs. Pollifax's friend peered out from the rear, lifted his brows in surprise at seeing her and walked grudgingly toward her. "Yes?" he asked curtly.

"The vest," said Mrs. Pollifax. "I ordered a brown sheep skin vest." She fumbled in her purse for paper.

"I know, I know," he said flatly. "I remember."

But Mrs. Pollifax nevertheless handed him the sales slip. "This one," she explained, moving to his side and pointing to the order. "I find I must have it sooner than I expected."

On it she had printed in pencil: MUST SEE TSANKO AT ONCE. URGENT.

The man looked at her sharply.

"Something has come up," she said clearly. "Can you rush the order?"

He handed the slip of paper back to her. "I see what can be done. You are lady at the hotel?"

"The Rila, yes."

"How soon do you leave?"

"As soon as I have the vest."

He nodded. "I will let you know," he said, and she left.

This time Debby submitted her passport at the hotel and registered legally, receiving a room of her own down the hall, which she left as quickly as possible to rejoin Mrs. Pollifax. It was she who opened the door to the tailor a few hours later. He carried a handsome vest on a hangar, unwrapped so that Mrs. Pollifax could see that it was brown. He handed her the bill, bowed and quickly walked away down the hall.

But it was not a bill, it was a note. BE AT SIDE ENTRANCE 7:15, WATCH FOR BLUE CAR. To this had been added in script, *Why does a man who raises geese carry in a valise a coat identical to yours?*

"Well, that's a punch line," Debby said when Mrs. Pollifax passed the message to her. "What does it mean? And—good heavens, what's the matter?"

Mrs. Pollifax had abruptly sat down on the edge of the bed. "An exact duplicate," she said in a startled voice. She was remembering her first night in Sofia, and the burglar who had arrived in the middle of her nightmare. She had discovered him with her quilted brown coat in his arms, yet at the same time her coat had been locked away securely in the closet. Supernatural powers indeed! There were *two* coats, and the burglar had brought the second coat into the room *with* him.

But why?

At that moment—with dizzying clarity—Mrs. Pollifax found her thoughts going back to Miss Hartshorne and a jammed door lock. *Of course he was heading for your apartment, Emily, he was carrying your brown quilted coat with him. I could see it plainly through the cellophane wrapping.*

Very softly Mrs. Pollifax said, "I have a distinct feeling that Mr. Carstairs wasn't frank with me this time. Debby —hand me those scissors on the bureau, will you?" Reaching for her coat, she looked it over, turned it inside out and stared at the lining.

"What are you going to do?" Debby asked in an alarmed voice, handing her the scissors.

"Operate," said Mrs. Pollifax and, grasping the lining of the coat, she began snipping the threads of one of the plump quilted squares.

"Are you out of your skull?" gasped Debby.

"I'm solving a mystery. You like mysteries, don't you?"

"I used to until I came to Bulgaria."

"Well, here's a new one for you." From her coat she drew a folded piece of paper and held it up.

"Money?" said Debby in a shocked voice.

"Some kind of foreign money." She turned over the note, frowning. "Not Bulgarian. Russian, do you suppose?"

Debby brought out a Bulgarian *lev* and compared them. "Not Bulgarian. Mrs. Pollifax, you didn't *know* about this? Do you suppose every single quilted square in your coat has a bill like this?"

"I think we can count on it," she said, and was silent, considering the situation.

"But why? And what are you going to do with the money now that you've found it?"

A faint smile tugged at Mrs. Pollifax's lips. "Since Mr. Carstairs didn't enlighten me, I see no need to do anything at all. I think I shall regard it as 'found money.' Finders keepers, you know."

"But there could be a small fortune here!"

Mrs. Pollifax nodded. "It's almost the hand of Providence intervening, isn't it?" she said cheerfully. "I always say it's an ill wind that doesn't blow someone good."

"Mrs. Pollifax, you're being mysterious."

"Yes, I am," she acknowledged truthfully. "But now it's time to go and meet Tsanko, and we mustn't keep the blue car waiting."

As Mrs. Pollifax and Debby advanced from the hotel steps to the curb the small blue car drew up, a young man leaned over to open the door for them and they climbed quickly into the rear seat. For fifteen minutes they toured the streets of Sofia and Mrs. Pollifax noted how frequently their driver checked his rearview mirror. Once he parked on a side street to allow cars to pass before he maneuvered out again to resume driving. It was half an hour before he abruptly pulled into a long alley, drove the length of it to an inside court, cut the engine and gestured toward a door ahead of them.

It was a rear door to a low, concrete-block warehouse. There were other warehouses and other doors emptying into the yard, all of them dark. Their escort unlocked the drab metal door with his own key and beckoned them to follow. They descended broad cement stairs and walked across an echoing expanse of floor piled high with wooden crates in neat rows. At the far end a door opened, emitting light, and Tsanko observed their arrival.

"Well, Amerikanski," he said humorously.

"Well, Tsanko," she said warmly.

"I was not sure I would see you again. I know that bad news brings you, but still I am delighted."

"Very bad news," Debby interrupted breathlessly. "They released Phil—cameras and newsmen and everything—and it wasn't Phil at all."

Tsanko nodded. "Yes, I learn this as soon as I returned to Sofia this afternoon. I learn more, too. Georgi—you have met Georgi? He is student at our university."

"Hi," Debby said.

Tsanko gave the young man instructions that sent him ahead into the room from which he'd emerged. Yet when they followed him inside the room was empty, which startled Mrs. Pollifax.

"We talk here, please." He pulled out wooden crates and they each claimed one.

"We meet in strange places," observed Mrs. Pollifax. "A cave, a furnace room—"

"About Phil," said Debby impatiently.

Tsanko began speaking, but without looking at Debby, which Mrs. Pollifax thought ominous. "As I told you this morning, General Ignatov is in charge of this nasty situation now, and General Ignatov is a man of much resource. He has produced another Trenda—a stroke of genius, is it not?"

"But how?" asked Mrs. Pollifax.

"There is this young man, of a same physiological character, a promising young man highly trained in the Soviet Union to speak English, to accomplish various matters, but with the great misfortune to have become addicted to cocaine. You understand? A grave embarrassment." Tsanko glanced at his watch. "He is just now landing in Belgrade to meet your press. He will be taken to a hotel. Tomorrow morning he will have performed usefully for his country—he will be found dead in his bed of a heart seizure."

"Oh no," she said sadly.

"Thus Philip Trenda will have been disposed of—*but not in Bulgaria*. Already it has been suggested to the senior Mr. Trenda in your United States that this is not his son. He knows, you understand? He will announce his departure for Europe to recover the body of his son. In truth he will proceed to Zurich to deposit the ransom money in a number account on Monday morning." He stopped, still not looking at Debby.

"And Phil? They'll release Phil then?" she asked in a hopeless voice.

Tsanko met her glance squarely at last, and after a terrible moment Debby covered her face with her hands.

"How did you find out all this?" asked Mrs. Pollifax quietly.

He didn't reply; he said instead, "You see the situation. To free your friend would make too many Philip Trendas."

There was silence, and then Mrs. Pollifax said in a stifled voice, "He'll never see America again, then. He'll die here?"

"Yes."

"But he's alive *now?*"

"Until Monday, when the ransom has been paid."

He had never wanted to come to Bulgaria and now he would meet his death here. He couldn't be more than twenty, she thought, and by Monday night he would be another statistic, another human being sacrificed to an insane political end. She thought of Philip's father preparing to leave for Zurich, understanding the odds but praying that somehow his son might be allowed to live. She said, "His father will be hoping for a miracle."

"There are no miracles in Bulgaria," Tsanko told her. "Someone has said that in my country a happy ending is a battle where only five thousand Bulgars are sacrificed to save a hundred Turks or Russians."

"Then we must make a miracle," said Mrs. Pollifax fiercely. "Surely we can make a miracle? Just to stand by and let this happen . . ." She looked at Tsanko. "Your Underground group is somewhere nearby, aren't they? Would you let me speak to them?"

Tsanko gave her a quick, startled glance. "You are always a surprise to me, Amerikanski. Yes, they are in the next room. They expect a report from me tonight about the passports."

"I have a proposition to make to them."

"Proposition? I do not know this word."

"Let me put it this way. You mentioned a mental hospital in Sofia."

"Panchevsky Institute, yes."

"You said that several of your friends are there now. I happen to believe Philip's there, too. That gives us a mutual interest in that prison, doesn't it? And you have an Underground."

His jaw dropped. "My dear Amerikanski, if you mean what I think you mean—"

"There's the other factor, the political one," she continued determinedly. "You don't approve of General Ignatov—you said so—but if he succeeds with the ransom and with Philip's murder then there'll be no stopping him, isn't that true?"

Tsanko stared at her from under his heavy brows. "You continue to surprise me, Amerikanski!"

Debby said, "Mrs. Pollifax, he seems to know, but I don't. *What are you talking about?*"

Neither of them answered her. With an effort Tsanko wrenched his gaze from Mrs. Pollifax's face. "You had better meet my 'Underground' before you develop ideas," he said dryly, and he arose and moved behind the furnace. There he opened a small steel door and led them into a room that resembled a ship's boiler room, its walls an abstract of crisscrossing pipes.

Four people turned to look at them in surprise. There was Kosta, whom they had last seen in Tarnovo, and Georgi, who had brought them here, and two other men, both of Tsanko's vintage. "This is all?" said Mrs. Pollifax, startled.

"We are only amateurs—concerned citizens," explained Tsanko. "We have never been militant revolutionists. It simply grew too much for us, seeing innocent friends threatened, misunderstood and sent to prison. Allow me to introduce you, putting aside last names, please. First I would like you to meet my old friend, Volko."

Volko arose, beaming at her. He was very tall, a charmingly pear-shaped gentleman whose narrow shoulders sloped down to a swelling stomach hung with a gold watch chain. He wore a black suit and a stiff white collar. She'd not seen anyone dressed like that since her childhood, and then it had been a costume shared by bank presidents and morticians. He looked very proper, very dignified, but there was a sardonic glint to his black eyes that promised a sense of the absurd. "I am so much honored," he said, very nearly clicking his heels as he bowed.

"Volko is the businessman in our group," Tsanko explained gravely. "As a matter of fact this is his warehouse."

"Volko," she murmured, smiling and shaking his hand. "And this is Boris."

"Boris! The man who warned Shipkov on the street?"

Boris, too, arose, but languidly. He looked like a man who nursed a chronic case of exhaustion—once erect he slouched as if the effort of standing had depleted him. Every line of his face drooped with irony and her exclamation of pleasure at meeting him caused him to flinch, as if he'd been met by an unexpectedly strong wind. But the grasp of his hand was surprisingly firm.

"Kosta you have already met," concluded Tsanko. "He has driven my car for me for many years." If he had expected comment on the smallness of his group he was disappointed; Mrs. Pollifax was the more intrigued by the fact that in a socialist state Tsanko had his own personal driver.

"Hi," said Debby, with a smile for Kosta.

"Does everyone speak English?" asked Mrs. Pollifax.

"All except Kosta."

"Perhaps then you could explain to them what I've just suggested to you?"

"What *have* you suggested?" asked Tsanko bluntly.

Everyone had sat down and now they all looked at her expectantly. It was not quite the same as addressing the

Garden Club at home, thought Mrs. Pollifax, and she anxiously cleared her throat. "I have an idea. A dangerous one," she admitted frankly. "I've brought you eight passports from America which you can't use because your friends have been taken to Panchevsky Institute. And there's Philip Trenda—only a pawn, you know, a young American student who's going to be murdered next week so that General Ignatov will keep his power. I think Philip's at Panchevsky Institute, too. Here are all these people imprisoned in the same building. I think we should get them out."

"Out?" echoed Debby in an awed voice.

"Out?" cried Georgi eagerly. "Oh—splendid!"

"Out," mused Volko thoughtfully. "Hmmmm."

"I have never heard such simplicity," murmured Boris. "Just—out?" He snapped his fingers.

"Yes."

Tsanko said, "Naturally we'd all enjoy very much rescuing our friends. Unfortunately none of us are magicians. No one escapes from Panchevsky Institute."

"Then perhaps it's time someone did," she said. "What on earth is an Underground for if you don't do things like that? I've never heard of an Underground just sitting around. They're supposed to . . ."

"To what?"

She gestured helplessly. "I don't know. *Do* things. Blow up trains, rescue people. That's what they do in movies."

"But this is not a movie," pointed out Tsanko logically.

"But who else can get them out? What *will* you do with your group?"

"Rescue people when possible, yes, but not blow up trains."

Mrs. Pollifax said, "I don't see why you can't rescue them while they're *in* prison. If we all put our heads together—"

"You are naïve," Tsanko told her bluntly.

"Not at all—I'm well aware of the risks and I'd insist upon sharing them. I've not come here empty-handed, either," she told him heatedly. "Did you know that Mrs. Bemish works at Panchevsky Institute? She works nights in the kitchen from eight o'clock to six in the morning, and don't forget that Philip is her nephew. She was utterly appalled to hear that he's here in prison because of her husband."

Tsanko said in astonishment, "You've seen her? You've told her?"

Mrs. Pollifax nodded. "Yes, of course, and I have every reason to believe she'll help us. I think I can also promise you the help of Assen Radev."

Tsanko looked at her in horror. "You know this Radev who followed you?"

"You explained him when you told me about the coat," she said. "I think he's a professional agent for the CIA."

The reaction to this was rewarding to say the least. Tsanko said incredulously, "How is this?"

"I at once opened up the lining of my coat to see why it's of such interest," she told him, and brought out the sample bill, handing it to him. "This is what I found. It seems I've brought rather a lot of money into your country without knowing it. I think Assen Radev was supposed to exchange coats with me very quickly and quietly. He certainly tried—he must have been my burglar."

Georgi said eagerly, "It is I who searched the valise. He walk around Sofia all the time carrying this bag. What a surprise, a coat so explicitly like yours."

"It was a surprise for me, too," said Mrs. Pollifax frankly.

"But this is Russian money," Tsanko said in surprise. She nodded.

He was considering this with a frown. "And even if Radev is a CIA agent it doesn't promise his help."

Mrs. Pollifax smiled at him forgivingly. "You might leave that to me," she suggested gently.

Tsanko turned to the others and they began speaking excitedly together in Bulgarian. When he turned back to Mrs. Pollifax he said, "Georgi is eager, as only young people can be. Kosta is gloomy, Volko interested and Boris—"

"Dismayed," said Boris heavily.

"Why?" asked Mrs. Pollifax.

He sighed. "I beg you to look at us, are we a group for violence? We have not even a gun among us. Have we?" he asked the others.

Volko said with a smile, "No, Boris."

"You see?"

Volko added pleasantly, "But you forget, comrade, that my factory makes Very pistols, parachute flares and fireworks. Such things are made of explosives."

"Splendid!" said Mrs. Pollifax, beaming at him.

Georgi said, "Boris, in class you teach us of violence, how is it you speak so negative now? You teach us how we fight the Turks and the Nazis—"

"But did I never point out we lose each time?" said Boris sarcastically.

Volko held up a hand. "Please, I would like to hear more of the Amerikanski's plan."

"Plan? How can there be a plan yet?" asked Mrs. Pollifax. "First we have to enlist Assen Radev and Mrs. Bemish, and then gather information about this Panchevsky Institute."

Tsanko said grimly, "This last I give you now. It is impregnable, an ancient building, a castle. The Turks did their torturing in it. It is a large, square, stone building in the middle of the city. Around it has been built a high stone wall with sentry boxes and lights at each corner of the wall. Streets go right past it . . ."

Mrs. Pollifax said thoughtfully, "Why don't we go and take a look at it right now? Is there a car available?"

The men exchanged glances. "Certainly not in a car," Tsanko murmured. "We must not be seen together."

"One of the trucks, perhaps?" said Volko. "There is one in the alley, a closed-up—how do you say, *van?* Georgi, you could wear coveralls and drive."

"*Ypa*," he said, grinning.

"It will be dangerous," said Boris. "My God, if we are stopped . . ."

Tsanko laughed and patted him on the shoulder. "Then the Amerikanski will rescue you, too, from Panchevsky Institute, my friend. Come, shall we go?"

17

Crouched in the rear of the van, Mrs. Pollifax watched their progress over Georgi's shoulder. It was early twilight. The lights of the cafes in the tourist district spilled out across the cobblestones along with the sound of strident nasal folk songs shouted into microphones that distorted the sound. A few people strolled along the pavement glancing into shop windows, but once they left the hotel area behind them all attempt at night life was abandoned and the streets were almost deserted.

They had driven for about ten minutes when Georgi said, "There it is ahead of us. The wall."

It loomed in the distance, an anachronism in this newly created suburban boulevard, an ugly Chinese wall cutting across their path, bisecting the road and forcing it to split to right and to left. The boulevard had a mild downhill grade. At the bottom Georgi braked in the shadow of the wall and turned, following it to the right. They came out in a broad square—"This is the front, the entrance," said Georgi—and Mrs. Pollifax peered over his shoulder at an expanse of flood-lit cobblestones, two shabby stone pillars embracing the iron gate, and a sentry's kiosk. Then the van passed, turning left to follow the wall down a narrow side street. On the opposite side from which they had entered the square, Georgi braked the van to a stop and they parked.

They were silent. The whole neighborhood was silent, as if crushed by this monstrosity of stone. Across this street on which they had parked, Mrs. Pollifax could look up at the wall as it rose fifteen or twenty feet above them. No actual light could be seen anywhere, yet an illumination like marsh mist hung over the compound, as though on the other side of the wall the sun had risen and it was noon.

"Damn," said Debby in a stifled, angry voice.

Mrs. Pollifax realized that Tsanko and the others were waiting for her to speak, their faces turned toward her, and she could think of nothing to say. Her eyes followed the wall down the street, picking out the silhouette of the sentry box mounted on the wall at the corner, where it turned at right angles. It was a relatively primitive sentry box, no more than an enclosure against rain or snow, its windows glassless and open; as far as she could see there were no sentries inside. "Drive around the corner, Georgi, let's look at the sentry box," she said.

Volko said, "We should not go around all the way again, we have been the only traffic on the square."

She nodded. "Once will do, surely."

The car moved, and now other heads peered to look at the sentry station, too; Mrs. Pollifax could still see no men inside, although as they continued slowly along the last side of the square they met a guard ambling along the top of the wall, a machine gun strapped to his back. Then they were again on the boulevard from which they had entered the square; Georgi accelerated the car and they sped up the boulevard.

"Well?" said Tsanko, leaning over, and his eyes were kind. "You are ready to give it up now?"

Mrs. Pollifax looked at him and then looked away, not answering. The sight of the wall had sobered her; she was still stricken by the visual impact of its height, length, solidity, but above all by its officialness. Nor was this lessened by the knowledge that it was only a wall. There was nothing rational about a wall, whether it encircled Berlin, San Quentin or the ghettos of Warsaw. A wall was a symbol, fortified as much by the idea behind it as by bricks and guns.

But she also remembered that inside this wall lived Philip Trenda, who was going to be killed in a few days. He was young and far from home and he had never wanted to come to Bulgaria, and Debby had said he liked Leonard Cohen and Simon and Garfunkel.

She said angrily, "I like Simon and Garfunkel, too. No, I'm not ready to give up, do you understand?"

They returned to the warehouse and sat down with cups of weak tea. The hot water was drawn from one of the furnace boilers by Volko, and Mrs. Pollifax shared three tea bags she carried in her purse. The silence proved oddly companionable. It was broken at last by Volko.

"This is not impossible, you know," he said thoughtfully. "The spirit counts for most. You recall, Tsanko and Boris, some of the tricks we play on the Nazis?"

"Twenty-eight years ago," put in Boris.

"*Da.* We have fewer muscles, but the more brains," pointed out Tsanko.

"You really have access to explosives?" Mrs. Pollifax asked Volko.

He made a gesture that encompassed the basement and the entire warehouse. "Access?" he said modestly. "Is all here. Mostly fireworks this month, enough for May Day in every socialist country."

"Well, now," said Mrs. Pollifax, her eyes brightening.

"For myself, I know a little karate. Debby, what could you contribute?"

Debby looked astonished. "You mean you'd let me help?"

"You'd have to," pointed out Mrs. Pollifax.

Debby considered this with great seriousness. "I wish I could think of something," she confessed. "I can drive a motorcycle. And I'm good on the parallel bars and the ropes, and come to think of it I know a lot about knots. All those years of summer camp, you know? Maybe I could tie up a guard."

Knots, motorcycle, wrote Mrs. Pollifax, pencil in hand.

They glanced next at Boris, who sat beside Debby looking glum. "Please," he said. "For this I know nothing."

"Come, come, Boris," said Tsanko, "you were once a champion at shooting. I see the gold medals on your wall."

"Really?" said Georgi eagerly.

Boris gave him a dark look. "What I shoot, Georgi, was the bow and the arrows."

"Oh," said Georgi dispiritedly.

"I am wondering," said Mrs. Pollifax thoughtfully, "if Panchevsky Institute's reputation may not be our greatest asset. In my experience this sort of thing induces carelessness." Fixing Boris with a stern eye, she said, "After all, if *you* had a reputation like that—terrifying—what else would you need? You could relax."

"Already you are terrifying *me*," Boris said. He smiled and the effect upon his gloomy features was dazzling. "I think you must be like one of our witches in the Balkan mountains."

"She thinks in a straight line," said Tsanko. "There are no detours in this woman. So. She has made a point—Panchevsky Institute may be impregnable, but human nature is not."

Volko glanced at his watch. "It grows late. I suggest

lists of what is available to us, and much careful thinking of this idea."

"And then when we've contacted Mrs. Bemish and Radev we can put them all together!" finished Mrs. Pollifax triumphantly. "In the meantime I'll volunteer to visit Assen Radev tomorrow. I can try to persuade Balkantourist to arrange a tour of his goose farm. You can tell me where it is and how to find it?" she asked Tsanko.

"It is the Dobri Vapcarow Collective farm, in the village of Dobri Vapcarow. You understand it is not *his* geese, this is socialist state. The geese are raised for their livers, which are one of our most successful exports to the Western world. For the making of *pâté de foie gras,*" he explained.

"How very capitalistic," murmured Mrs. Pollifax. "But I mustn't visit this goose farm with the money still in my coat. Is there a way to remove it overnight?"

"There is our tailor comrade," put in Volko.

"Good! And if the coat could be returned to me in the morning, quite early, at the Rila?"

"You give us a busy night again," said Tsanko, handing her a piece of paper. "This is the name of the collective. I have written it in Bulgarian and in English."

"What about Mrs. Bemish?" asked Debby. "She said she'd die for her brother."

"A momentary aberration, perhaps," commented Mrs. Pollifax. "But yes—what about Mrs. Bemish?"

"I know where she lives," said Georgi eagerly. "I could telephone her tomorrow to say I have message for her. Does she know yet her husband has been killed?"

Tsanko shook his head. "How can she know when he is buried in the rocks of Tsaravets Hill? Only Nikki will guess. But of course she will be alarmed by the absence, it has been twenty-four hours now."

Boris said, "You go and see this woman, Georgi, and she will tell the police about you and I will lose my best student."

"I'll take the chance," Georgi said fiercely. "Someone has to be liaison, like army."

Tsanko intervened with a sigh. "This is a problem for all of us. I have no desire to be seen by these two people, this Radev and Mrs. Bemish. You understand the danger for us if we can be identified?"

Debby said joyously, "Stocking masks!"

Mrs. Pollifax clapped her hands. "Bravo, Debby!" Seeing the others look blank, she explained. "This is what was first used in our Brink's holdups. The silk stocking over the head blurs the features completely. I can contribute several pairs, and you'll see."

"Holdups?" said Volko, puzzled. "Brink?"

Boris said firmly, "James Cagney, Volko. You recall the American movies we enjoy so much?"

Mrs. Pollifax checked her watch and stood up. "It's getting late," she said regretfully. "Debby and I should go back to the hotel before anyone wonders where we've gone. In any case, if I'm going to request a visit to a goose farm I'll have to telephone Balkantourist at once." She added sadly, "They don't seem to like sudden jolts."

It was agreed that the blue car would call for them at the hotel at five o'clock tomorrow. "Do not be discouraged, Amerikanski," Tsanko told her. "We are neither fools nor cowards. You give us hope."

It had been a long day and Mrs. Pollifax was looking forward to her first night of uninterrupted sleep since arriving in Bulgaria. She and Debby said good night in the hall and Mrs. Pollifax waited, watching, while Debby unlocked the door of her room, gave her a peace sign and went inside. Disguising a yawn—it was only half-past nine—she unlocked her own door.

The lights were on. Seated opposite the door in a chair was Nevena.

"Why, Nevena," said Mrs. Pollifax warmly, "just the person I wanted to see!"

"So, Mrs. Pollifax," said Nevena grimly.

It was at that moment that Mrs. Pollifax remembered the long list of her indiscretions with Balkantourist and the number of necessary apologies that had accumulated. She was relieved that Debby—whose presence in Bulgaria was still on tenuous grounds, as yet unrealized by both Eastlake and Balkantourist—was safely out of sight. "I was about to telephone Balkantourist," Mrs. Pollifax said truthfully.

"You were not in Tarnovo when the driver called for you at one o'clock this afternoon," said Nevena.

"No—I wasn't," admitted Mrs. Pollifax.

"He waited."

"I left a message—"

"He had orders to wait for you. He waited. Where were you?"

"I was offered a ride back to Sofia. Mr. Eastlake at my Embassy had telephoned—"

Nevena bluntly interrupted. "That we know. But"—she fixed her eyes sternly on Mrs. Pollifax—"Mr. Eastlake telephone you before I do."

Mrs. Pollifax blinked at this; Balkantourist had been doing some thorough detective work during the course of the day. Obviously she was in trouble here, which, with so many other things to think about, seemed tiresome indeed. "I offered to go by train," pointed out Mrs. Pollifax. "I expressed an interest in getting back to Sofia earlier than you suggested."

Nevena threw up her hands. "I never tour anybody like you. Balkantourist is angry, very angry. You do whatever you please, it is most insulting."

"I'm sorry."

"You are sorry, but you continue to do what you please. You not behave nicely. It is too much, we have no choice."

"No choice?" echoed Mrs. Pollifax, very alert now suddenly.

"You must go," Nevena said coldly, rising. "You go first plane tomorrow."

Mrs. Pollifax sat very still. She understood at last that her first battle was being fought here, in this room, and if she lost there would be no other battles at all. She felt a deep chill rising in her and she knew that she must use this cold to become ruthless, not for herself but for the thin hope of rescuing Philip Trenda. "I'm sorry," she said quietly to Nevena. "I'm really very sorry, Nevena. I was about to telephone you my apologies and ask if I might visit one of your great collectives, of which I've been hearing such splendid things. But of course if I must leave . . ." She sighed. "If Balkantourist says I must leave then of course I must. My daughter, Jane, will be disappointed, of course. She raises geese."

"She what?" said Nevena, startled.

"She raises geese," Mrs. Pollifax said firmly. "I have just heard this afternoon, Nevena, that your country is becoming well known for its *pâté de foie gras*. I had no idea. My daughter would be so interested in learning what your country . . ."

Nevena stared at her. "You never mention this in your letter to Balkantourist of what you wish to see."

Mrs. Pollifax shrugged. "I had no idea—I thought the French were the *pâté de foie gras* people. The Strasbourg *pâté de foie gras* is so . . . so . . ."

"French!" Nevena's lip curled. "French?" She tossed her head. "We excel the French, they are bourgeois. We export much goose livers for the best *pâté de foie gras*—"

"So I've just heard," murmured Mrs. Pollifax. "And I was looking forward—"

"The *French*," Nevena repeated contemptuously. She was silent a moment and then she said cautiously, "It is possible that if your apology is acceptable—I can see."

"It would certainly be merciful," said Mrs. Pollifax truthfully.

"Okay, I see," said Nevena. "If this is so, someone take

you tomorrow, which is Friday, and you leave Saturday morning."

"Without a tour of Sofia," said Mrs. Pollifax, nodding.

Nevena said sharply, "Without tour of Sofia? You have seen Sofia!"

Mrs. Pollifax shook her head. "Only Mount Vitosha, and then I became tired, you see, and returned to the hotel. I've not seen the Nefesky Cathedral, or your monument to the Soviet Army, or the Georgi Dimitrov Mausoleum. Or Lenin Square, for that matter."

Nevena's lips thinned. "You cannot be trusted with a car again." But she had not said no. A lengthy silence followed, which heartened Mrs. Pollifax because Nevena was frowning thoughtfully. After a moment she lifted her gaze and regarded Mrs. Pollifax sternly. "You have no sense," she said. "You come, you go, we cannot find you."

"True, Nevena," she said contritely.

"But you are old woman. I believe you when you say you are sorry. I make with you a compromise. If you behave very nice we take you tomorrow to collective farm. On Saturday ten o'clock you join organized tour—many peoples—of my city. Then you leave Saturday night seven o'clock sharp to reach airport nine o'clock plane."

Soberly Mrs. Pollifax nodded. She had at least gained forty-eight hours; it might be enough time, it had to be enough time.

"And," added Nevena severely, "you report to Balkantourist all the time. On such terms—"

"I'm on probation," suggested Mrs. Pollifax.

"Pro-bation? I not know such word."

"It means," explained Mrs. Pollifax, "that I have behaved very rudely and am being given a second opportunity for which I am most grateful, Nevena."

Nevena's face softened. "You are not *bad*, she explained, as though she had considered this already in some depth. "But you are careless, lazy. In Bulgaria peoples are not careless and lazy."

Mrs. Pollifax nodded; she believed her.

"We give you forty-eight hours, no more. But I—how you call it?—intercede for you because you are not bad, only without sense. But you make sense now, you understand? Be very, very good or you go."

"Thank you, Nevena," said Mrs. Pollifax.

"You see? We are reasonable peoples, we Bulgarians," Nevena said, touching her almost affectionately on the shoulder. "In our anger we can be kind."

"Very kind," said Mrs. Pollifax firmly, and hoped she would leave soon.

"The Dobri Vapcarow Collective raises geese for the *pâté de foie gras*," Nevena said. "At nine sharp be in lobby."

When she had gone Mrs. Pollifax fumbled for the slip of paper Tsanko had given her upon which he had written the name of the collective at which Radev worked: it was the Dobri Vapcarow Collective, and Mrs. Pollifax decided that her fortune, however mixed so far, was at least for the moment on the ascendency.

18

Debby was in Mrs. Pollifax's room at seven. "I thought I'd want to sleep all day, but there's too much going on," she explained. "Mrs. Pollifax, were you serious last night? I mean, do you think there's the slightest *possibility?*"

Mrs. Pollifax groped for pencil and paper and wrote, *Room may be bugged. Wait.* Handing it to Debby, she said casually, "My Balkantourist guide, Nevena, was waiting for me here last night. Balkantourist feels I've behaved very irresponsibly toward them—as of course I have," she added piously. "Nevena had come to suggest I leave Bulgaria at once."

"They're expelling you?" gasped Debby.

"That word was not mentioned, fortunately—it sounds a little strong. However, she's graciously given me another forty-eight hours—if I behave myself—so that I can visit a collective farm today, and tour Sofia tomorrow."

"Well, wow," Debby said, making congratulatory gestures.

Mrs. Pollifax nodded. "And now I shall take a bath."

"I just might write a postcard to Dr. Kidd," said Debby.

"I'll tell him I've eloped with a Bulgarian sheepherder."

Mrs. Pollifax closeted herself in the bathroom and blessed the sufficiency of hot water in Sofia: she had a great deal of thinking to do, mainly about Debby, who had been so conveniently overlooked by everyone for the moment. Debby's thumb was healing now, they were back in Sofia, but somehow, through circumstances beyond anyone's control, Debby had become more and more involved during the last twenty-four hours. The problem was, how much more involved should she become?

Her being here in Sofia was dangerous. There was Nikki, who by this time would have guessed something untoward had happened to Mr. Bemish on Wednesday night. Nikki would be asking questions. Inquiries in Tarnovo would take time; they would, however, establish the fact that not only had Mrs. Pollifax survived her trip to Tarnovo but that she had left Tarnovo alive yesterday and accompanied by a young American girl with long brown hair.

Of course there was no way to link them with Bemish in Tarnovo. The black Renault would be discovered parked on a main street in town, and the bodies of Bemish and Titko Yugov would probably never be found. But there would remain the unalterable coincidence that all of them had been in Tarnovo the same night, and that Bemish had disappeared while Mrs. Pollifax was still very much alive. It would also prove very dismaying for Nikki to learn that Debby was her companion; he wouldn't like this. He would look for them in Sofia and place them under surveillance again. By tonight at the latest, she mused; we've had a day's respite, that's all.

But Nikki was such an angry young man that it was unpleasant to contemplate his reactions. Their unexpected survival would certainly curb his delight at how smoothly his plot was moving toward its climax in Zurich on Monday morning.

And if he ever learned that both she and Debby had

been at the Embassy yesterday to witness the release of Philip's impersonator—she shuddered. It could become very difficult for them to remain alive in Bulgaria.

Should she suggest that Debby leave, then? She thought that if she insisted upon it Debby might consent to go as far as Belgrade and wait for news, but she would certainly rebel at going any farther. The trouble here was that Debby might talk too much in a changed environment. Belgrade would still be buzzing with gossip about Philip Trenda's release and Debby would be eager to find other young companions again. The temptation to tell what she knew would be very strong indeed.

But the worst of it, reflected Mrs. Pollifax, would be Debby's terrible vulnerability in Belgrade. Nikki had already found his way there once and he presumably still owned a valid passport for travel. Who would there be to watch over Debby?

This last realization settled it: it might be dangerous for Debby here in Sofia; it could prove equally dangerous for her to be banished to a nearby capital where Mrs. Pollifax could no longer keep an eye on her. *I'll ask Tsanko about hiding her for the next forty-eight hours,* she thought, and made a mental note to see that Debby recovered her passport from the hotel today.

"The tailor delivered your coat," Debby announced as Mrs. Pollifax emerged from her thoughts and her bath. "The receipt's on the bed."

Mrs. Pollifax picked up the receipt and read *Money in coat is counterfeit*. "What on earth!" she exclaimed.

Debby nodded. "Your—uh—employers are certainly weirdos."

"Devious," said Mrs. Pollifax. "Rather shocking, too, I might add." She wondered if Assen Radev knew the Russian rubles were counterfeit. Probably. Counterfeit money did upsetting things to a country's economy, didn't it? If enough counterfeit Russian money circulated through a devoted satellite country it could cause some rather hard feelings toward Russia, couldn't it? The bills would move steadily out from Sofia into the villages and among the peasants, who distrusted paper money anyway, and if a hard-working peasant sold a precious cow and found his currency was worthless it would prove quite a blow. In fact it would be heartbreaking, she thought with a shake of her head. She would have to speak very sternly to Carstairs about this when they met again. Then she remembered that Carstairs would probably have a number of biting comments to make about her involving the Underground in unauthorized activities and she decided not to think about it now and began looking for a clean pair of gloves.

"And what kind of mash have we here?" asked Mrs. Pollifax in a depressed voice as she peered into still another tub at the Dobri Vapcarow Collective.

She and Debby had been at the collective for nearly two hours and had not so much as glimpsed Assen Radev. They had seen a great number of geese, and rather too much of their substitute guide. He was a young man named Slavko, who sweated heavily over his translations, but she supposed it was not every day that a guide was forced into translating words like force-fed, *foie gras*, liver, mash and gaggles of geese.

"This mixture has more corn than rye or wheat," said Slavko after conferring with the foreman. He had already explained that the Dobri Vapcarow Collective was such a success that it was now a model for other collectives, and a laboratory for small experiments. "They eat our *foie gras* in all the capitals of Europe," Slavko said proudly. "It brings much praise, much money."

The foreman, who spoke no English, listened impassively. He was a huge, ruddy-faced man in overalls and muddy hip boots who seemed to regard Slavko with the amusement he would accord a three-legged goose or some other colorful mutation of animal life; he smiled occasionally at Mrs. Pollifax, frequently at Debby and not at all at Slavko.

But of Assen Radev they had seen nothing, and Mrs. Pollifax began to fear that she had miscalculated. She'd had no real, graspable idea of what a collective farm was, vaguely assuming it to resemble a New Jersey truck farm, intimate and on a small scale. This collective was like an open sea of land with a small island of barns on it. The cluster of barns and outbuildings was separated by smaller seas of trampled mud, and totally surrounded by pens of geese, but beyond this nothing could be seen on the horizon except clouds, and field after field of growing corn and wheat: the collective incorporated three villages and mile after mile of land. Assen Radev could be anywhere; he was certainly not here.

"The land belongs to the workers," Slavko was reciting. "After the crops are harvested, twenty percent of the profits go to the state, ten percent to the planting and ten percent to new machinery and repairs. The remaining sixty percent is divided among the workers according to workdays they have given—for two hundred workdays one thousand *leva*, for two hundred and fifty workdays, fifteen hundred *leva*."

"That's five hundred American dollars," Debby announced triumphantly.

"In this room," continued Slavko after consulting with the foreman, "there is compared the feeding by the hand with the feeding by machine."

Debby peered into the room and stepped back. "Ech," she said. She had barely survived watching the geese fed by machine. She had fled outside, where Mrs. Pollifax had heard her retching. "I won't," she said. "I can't."

Mrs. Pollifax nodded. "Quite sensible. Wait outside."

Four healthy-looking young women in overalls looked up as they entered the next room of the barn. Each was engaged in inserting a funnel down the throat of a goose, emptying mash into the funnel and then forcing it down the goose's throat with a milking motion of the hands. They worked quickly, contentedly, like laboratory workers moving from test tube to test tube.

"It's only if you don't think about it, I suppose," said Mrs. Pollifax vaguely, and Slavko looked at her questioningly. "Forcing the food into them like that," she explained.

"It makes beautiful livers—big, big," Slavko said, reverently sketching dimensions with his hands.

Mrs. Pollifax looked away quickly, certain that she would never be able to eat *pâté de foie gras* again.

"Now we have the big surprise for you," Slavko said as they emerged into the sunlight again. "Please—across these ditches—step high!—to last building."

"Another surprise?" said Debby wearily, catching up with them.

They mounted the wooden steps of a building with curtains at its windows, and entered a large bare room. "Please—you relax now if you please," said Slavko. "This is building of collective meetings and keeping of books. Please sit, remove the coats if you will and relax."

"I will," said Mrs. Pollifax, and shrugged off her coat and hung it over a chair, sitting down next to it to guard it.

But when the foreman arrived, moving more slowly than they, Slavko hurried them all into a second room. "See—for you!" he cried with pleasure.

Mrs. Pollifax exclaimed aloud. A long trestle table had been set up in this room and on it had been spread for them the fruits of the farm: bowls of fat red raspberries still glistening with dew; platters of delicate honeydew, chunks of cantaloupe and red juicy watermelon, a small loaf of *pâté* and several jugs of colorless liquor. At once Slavko slipped into the role of host and handed Debby and Mrs. Pollifax tiny glasses into which he poured the liquid.

"Slivowicz," he said, beaming.

"How very hospitable of you all," she said. Over his

shoulder Mrs. Pollifax met the interested gaze of Lenin mounted on the wall: the picture was the only decorative note in the meeting room. "To peace," she added, lifting her glass, and suddenly remembering that she had left her coat in the other room. "My coat," she said. "Debby, could you . . .?"

"Right," said Debby, and promptly left, but when she returned she was empty-handed and obviously puzzled. She mutely shook her head, shrugging, and Mrs. Pollifax had to continue listening to the statistics that Slavko was earnestly reciting, as though by sheer volume he could persuade her of Bulgaria's superiority.

At last she turned to Debby and said bluntly, "Not there?"

"Absolutely vanished."

Slavko pressed more *slivowicz* on them, but Mrs. Pollifax demurred, her mind now on the missing coat. "Liquid fire," she told Slavko, smiling, and then, "I do think we must leave, Slavko. We're growing tired." And late, she added silently, noting that already it was two o'clock. Thanking them all with enthusiasm, she made her retreat to the anteroom and on the threshold stopped short because her coat was hanging over the chair where she had left it.

She and Debby exchanged glances. Without any change of expression Mrs. Pollifax picked up her coat and put it on; her heart was beating faster. She had filled its pockets before coming here and she was not surprised to find her handkerchief still in the left pocket and a handful of coins in the right. What her fingers searched for now were the small knots of thread that she had sewn into the lining of the left pocket: five of them, thick enough to be felt but not seen. And they were no longer there.

"What is it?" asked Debby in a low voice as they walked toward the car.

Mrs. Pollifax was smiling. "I'm daring to hope that our trip here hasn't been in vain."

"Even though you didn't see him?"

"Not a glimpse," she said, "but I think I'm wearing the other coat."

They had not seen Radev at the collective, but when Mrs. Pollifax unlocked the door of her hotel room her burglar of the first evening was sitting in a chair by the window. "You certainly made good time," she congratulated him, closing and locking the door behind her.

His brows lifted. "You are not surprised?"

"No, of course not. I do hope I didn't hurt you too badly the other night?"

His gaze was stony. "I have come for the money—it was not in the coat. I will have it now, please."

"If the money had been in the coat," she said reasonably, "you wouldn't have come and I would never have met you. I want to talk to you. By the way, the room may be bugged."

"The hell it is," said Radev. "I checked." He regarded her with curiosity, his eyes hostile. "You're not the amateur I first thought, but this is bad, very bad, this meeting. Against all orders."

"I first met you as a burglar," she retorted, "and that wasn't *my* idea."

"You give me helluva shock. In fact you give me helluva lot of shocks. How can I get near you when the secret police stay on your tail—and I mean really on your tail—from seven o'clock Monday on? I never have a chance. Then you go off to Borovets but are not at Borovets at all. Now I am waiting for my money." He brought a small pistol from his pocket and rested it casually on one knee.

"Did you know the Russian rubles are counterfeit?" she asked, sitting on the bed opposite him.

"Sure I know they're counterfeit. How did *you* know they're counterfeit?"

"I think that gun is extremely bad manners," said Mrs. Pollifax, glancing at it. "Do you mind pointing it in another direction? We're supposed to be allies, you know."

"It's so you don't get any ideas, and don't be too sure we're allies, either," he said. "I got no allies, I work for cash. And I want that money."

"And we want *you*," Mrs. Pollifax told him cheerfully. "You're a professional, you see, and we need one badly." Operation sounded like a professional word. "We have an operation planned."

He said savagely, "Appendix or tonsils? Look, lady, I'm in a hurry and I want that money. Do I have to kill you to get it?"

Mrs. Pollifax shrugged. "Possibly. Have you heard of Philip Trenda?"

"Sure I've heard of Philip Trenda. He's dead. They found him dead today in Belgrade."

"So soon?" murmured Mrs. Pollifax. "That poor boy. Except it wasn't Philip Trenda who died in Belgrade, you see, it was an imposter. Philip Trenda's still alive and in Sofia."

Radev sighed. "Lady, I couldn't care less. I'm not paid to worry about Trenda, I'm paid to get that money you brought in."

Mrs. Pollifax said tactfully, "But you see, I have it and you don't."

He stared at her in astonishment. "You're blackmailing me?"

"I wondered how long it would take you to understand," she said happily. "Of course I'm blackmailing you. I have what you want, and you have what I want. That's the way blackmail works, isn't it? But I'll be very glad to give you the rubles after you've volunteered to help."

"Volunteered?" he said mockingly.

"Yes, volunteered."

"And if I take my lumps and just leave?"

"Why should you?" she asked. "We only want to borrow your professional services for a few days. You'll have the rubles by Sunday." *If we're still alive,* she added silently.

"Christ," he muttered. "Maybe I ought to shoot you and forget the whole thing."

"The others, of course, would know that you shot me. I wouldn't give a nickel for your chances of survival."

"Others?"

"The people I'm working with," she told him. "The Underground that I'm allied with here."

"You're kidding me. In Bulgaria?"

"It's my assignment, contacting them. It's they who identified you when you were following me, and they who searched your bag and found the duplicate coat. They know all about you. Name, address and—uh—affiliations."

"Christ," he groaned. "All right, help do what?"

"Free Philip Trenda, of course, as well as a few friends of the Underground."

He considered, scowling. "And then I'd get the rubles?"

"Then you'd get the rubles."

"And where are these people?"

"In Panchevsky Institute."

He sprang to his feet. "For chrissake, why not choose something easy? Like assassinating the Premier, for instance."

"Please—I do not like profanity," begged Mrs. Pollifax.

"Are you out of your mind? Panchevsky Institute?"

"Since that's where he is—and since we want to get him out," she said tartly, "then naturally that's the place from which we will have to recover him."

"Insane," he said. "When?"

"This weekend."

"For chrissake."

"Mr. Radev—"

"Okay, sorry, but I tell you it's impossible, you're mad. I got a contact at Panchevsky who tells me about security and it's tight, it's—"

"Contact?" said Mrs. Pollifax quickly. "A prisoner?"

"Of course not, a guard," he snapped. "What do you

think I am, an amateur? He tells me who goes in, who comes out—for a price, of course, but he also tells me—"

"Mr. Radev, I love you," said Mrs. Pollifax impulsively, and leaned over and kissed him. "You see? You know a guard. I *knew* you'd be able to help us."

Radev recoiled. "Keep your hands off me, lady. For chrissake."

"I'm just so pleased," she confessed. "The others lack a certain toughness, a certain experience—and you even have a gun."

He looked alarmed. "You mean they *don't?*"

"It's almost five o'clock," she said, consulting her watch. "I suggest you come along and meet them now. We've very little time, and final plans simply have to be made tonight."

Still he stood, not moving. "I have one thing to say," he announced. "You look like a nice old lady. Really nice. Really kind, sweet, gentle. You are not nice," he added.

"Now *that*," said Mrs. Pollifax, "is one of the nicest compliments I've had from a professional. Thank you, Mr. Radev."

"Oh for chrissake," he said bitterly.

19

This time when the small blue car drew up to the Hotel Rila, Mrs. Pollifax directed Georgi to the hotel's service entrance. "Assen Radev is joining us by way of the rear door. He's just enlisted," she told him.

"*Bora,*" murmured Georgi, impressed. "You really are like a witch. But he will have to wear bandage over the eyes or he will know to find us again. Your scarf, please?"

"All right. What about Mrs. Bemish?"

"She has been with us all day giving much information. This lady has much courage. Last night she go to third floor at Panchevsky Institute—very illegitimate, you understand—and looks. She make guards very angry, but she says, 'This is Petrov's son.' "

"I'm so glad we went to see her," said Debby.

Radev climbed in and grudgingly suffered the scarf to be tied over his eyes. When they arrived at the warehouse, their steps echoing again through the basement, Georgi whispered, "You have face stockings?"

Mrs. Pollifax handed him four pairs of stockings and he hurried ahead. When she and Debby and Radev entered the room behind the furnace they found the faces of their Underground friends unrecognizably blurred: the noses flattened, mouths distorted and chins obscured by the gauzy stockings. Mrs. Pollifax removed Radev's blindfold and he swore heavily. "Goons!" he cried despairingly.

"Bring in Mrs. Bemish," said Tsanko. He was lifting a large sheet of cardboard to the wall. When he had propped it among the pipes he stood back and Mrs. Pollifax saw that it was a large diagram of Panchevsky Institute. "Good evening," he said, bowing. "I look sinister? As you can see, we have been busy."

"Good evening, Tsanko. We've been busy, too. This is Assen Radev, who knows a guard at Panchevsky Institute."

"Someone's missing," she said, counting the shrouded heads.

"Capital!"

"Volko—he has been taking apart fireworks today and working out formulas. Is most important. Ah, Mrs. Bemish," he said.

Georgi had brought in Mrs. Bemish, looking frightened, although her face brightened at sight of Mrs. Pollifax and Debby. "They think I do something," she whispered to Mrs. Pollifax. "Is this possible?"

"Ah—here is Volko, we begin now," said Tsanko. "Please, everyone sit? Please, the meeting is to come to order," he said sternly. "We are about to consider the storming of Panchevsky."

Boris said sourly, "What a pity we not forget whole thing and go to big tourist nightclub for evening."

Tsanko leaned over and affectionately gripped his shoulder. Straightening, he said, "Perhaps I say now that Boris has twice been to prisons for slips of the tongue. He has spent eight of past sixteen years in jails for mention of history not in our Republic of Bulgaria textbooks. Yet still he risks himself by helping us."

"I am behaving so badly you must say this?" asked Boris gloomily.

"Very badly," Tsanko told him gravely.

Boris smiled, and again his face lighted up. "Then I be quiet—if only someone tell me how to silence my stomach, which growls at thought of prisons. Never mind, as history professor I have always the longing to see history made. Please continue."

Tsanko nodded. "Mrs. Bemish has brought much news for us tonight, both good and bad. In return we have had only bad news for her. We have told her that her husband is dead. Because his death is on our heads it is only fair we give her passport to leave country if this experience is survived. It is agreed? . . . Now here is diagram made from her very helpful description."

After swift glances at Mrs. Bemish they turned to the diagram. "The bad news is this," continued Tsanko. "Our Bulgarian friends are here"—he pointed to the first floor of the south side. "Philip Trenda is at opposite end of Panchevsky, and high up, on third floor."

"Ouch," said Debby, wincing.

Glances swerved reproachfully to Mrs. Pollifax. "And the good news?" she asked, ignoring the others.

Mrs. Bemish spoke. "The wall is not busy," she said. "Only one man walk round and round. This is vacation season, workers go free to Varna and Golden Sands. Seven guards gone this week."

"Do you mean there aren't sentries in each box?"

Mrs. Bemish nodded.

"A touch of carelessness," murmured Mrs. Pollifax happily.

"What are the plans?" asked Assen Radev, speaking for the first time.

Mrs. Pollifax said, "We make the plans now. To begin with, because it does look so frightful—the diagram—I suggest we forget it's a prison with a wall around it and look at it as though it's two boxes, one inside the other."

Assen Radev made a rude sound.

Boris said, "We are attacking *boxes?*"

"But she's right," Debby said, jumping to her feet. "Look where Phil is, his cell is high up but directly across from the wall."

"Three stories high," pointed out Boris.

"Yes, but don't you see? We wouldn't have to enter the prison at all to rescue Phil if we could get across the courtyard from the wall to a window."

Boris sighed. "And which of us has wings? Who is an angel? What windows would be open in a prison?"

Debby said impatiently, "I don't know about windows, but I do know you can get across space like that with ropes. I told you I know about ropes. Last summer at camp we learned how to cross white water—that's rapids —on a rope. It was a survival course, only our parents heard about it and the instructor got fired and we all went back to beadwork. But what's the difference between crossing rapids or a prison courtyard by rope?"

"Did you do it personally?" asked Mrs. Pollifax. "Can you remember how it worked?"

Debby nodded. "Yes to both."

Tsanko shook his head. "You are forgetting something. Doubtless your instructor swam the rapids first to secure the rope at the other side. How would you achieve this across a courtyard?"

With a heavy sigh Boris uncrossed his legs. Almost crossly he said, "Do not obliterate the child. I hesitate to encourage this madness, but the solution is there—the rope could be shot across with the bow and the arrow." He sat back and glared at them all.

"Hey," said Debby, looking with a fresh eye at Boris.

"Wild," said Assen Radev disgustedly.

"Of course it's wild," Mrs. Pollifax told him indignantly. "What else have we to work with but imagination?"

"Okay, you want wild ideas? I have the wild idea," said Volko, sitting up and walking to the diagram. "Here on first floor you see our countrymen, our friends. Let us look at them a minute. You recall this is hill here, on Persenk Boulevard. If one of my trucks is stolen, with explosives in it, and is parked here on Persenk Boulevard, at top of hill, and brakes happen to be bad, very bad, and the truck begin rolling . . ."

There was silence.

Georgi said, "It would roll down the hill and explode the outer wall but go no farther. It would never touch the walls of Panchevsky."

"Explosives? You have explosives?" said Assen Radev. "Me, I have only geese and one pistol. If you have dynamite here is what could be done."

As Assen rose from his chair Mrs. Pollifax wrote down *geese—one pistol.*

"You need two explosions, two separate ones, you understand? One for outside wall, one for Institute. What kind of explosives you have?"

"Fireworks," said Boris gloomily.

"You're kidding. What about detonators?"

"A small amount of pentolite," said Volko. "But not enough for two big explosions."

Radev frowned. "On collective there is PETN for clearing of rocks. But what do I get from this?" he demanded. "For me this is very dangerous, I know none of you, but you all know who I am. Anytime it pleases, you need just finger me, telling identity, what I do."

Tsanko nodded. "He has a point there."

Mrs. Pollifax realized that to her growing list of indiscretions she had added the lifting of an agent's cover. She sighed.

Radev said, "You give this lady here, this Mrs. Bemish, passport out of country. I think I prefer passport to counterfeit Russian rubles."

The members of the Underground exchanged glances.

"We have only eight passports," pointed out Tsanko. "We've promised Mrs. Bemish safe-conduct to her brother and we reserve one for this young Trenda, who will not have a passport any more, and there are four of our countrymen who must not remain in Bulgaria."

"That's six," Radev said. "Give me one and you keep fifty thousand counterfeit Russian rubles in trade."

Tsanko and Volko exchanged amused glances. Volko said, "We might have a use for those counterfeit rubles, eh, my friend?"

"But it leaves us with only one passport." Tsanko turned to Radev. "You would have to earn it. Let us hear first what you can do to earn it."

Radev laughed. "You get money's worth from me—I know explosives. I learn in America before they deport me. I am real hood, and frankly do not care to see another goose in my life again. I know also the guard at Panchevsky named Miroslav. You give some counterfeit rubles and I pay him well for whatever you wish him to do. Maybe he even let me into Panchevsky, yes? A little explosive wrapped in plastic, a fuse, and I maybe break locks here or there. All this I do for passport."

His words brought a distinct change to the atmosphere. Radev was just what they needed. Mrs. Pollifax could sense doubts being replaced by eagerness.

Even Mrs. Bemish was affected. Leaning forward, she said with bright eyes, "I go to work now, but first, you do this at night when I am there and I put out electric boxes if you show me how. In room off kitchen, big room. Electric switches run lights and siren."

"Sirens—*bora!*" muttered Georgi.

"*Da,* sirens."

"They have a generator for emergencies, I suppose," Tsanko said.

Mrs. Bemish nodded. "When electric go off—snowstorm or power kaput—big machine start. Generator."

"How long before they can start it?"

"I think," she said, and closed her eyes. "Two, maybe three years back. I am making mishmash. Elena bring candle and I cut maybe ten eggplants. Then I peel and take out seeds before generator bring lights again." She opened her eyes. "Ten, maybe fifteen minutes."

Georgi said, "You mean we have only ten minutes—fifteen at most—to get prisoners out?"

"You want to spend any longer in Panchevsky Institute?" said Boris dryly. "You hear her, we have ten eggplants' time."

Mrs. Pollifax intervened. "Another point. Difficult as it may be, I strongly urge that we do this tomorrow night or Sunday morning. I've been asked by Balkantourist to leave."

"How is this?" said Tsanko.

She told him of Nevena and her anger. "So I shall have to tour Sofia tomorrow and behave very well, which means assignments really must be distributed tonight."

"We prefer not to use women," Tsanko told her.

"Nonsense," she said flatly. "Everyone involved in this can't wear stocking masks over their faces. You're going to have to use people who have passports and can leave the country."

Radev said, "This is true. If you give me passport I risk myself big. This lady leave, too, and the girl. If this is success there will be investigation later."

Tsanko threw up his hands helplessly. "Then we must get to work—serious work!"

"Exactly," said Volko, "Let us hear more talk."

As everyone began to speak at once Mrs. Pollifax thought, Brainstorming! and settled back contentedly in her chair, knowing they were involved now, knowing that each of them was ready to make something happen.

It was midnight before they reached a tentative plan and broke up, but only because they needed sleep for the hours ahead. During her day as a tourist Mrs. Pollifax was to purchase nine Bulgarian wristwatches—one for each member of the group—so that the ten or fifteen minutes allotted them could be plotted precisely by the hands of identical watches. Debby was to drop out of sight, hidden by Georgi in an abandoned hut on the outskirts of the city. In that same hut in the country Volko and Radev would spend most of the day designing their explosives. Assen Radev was to contact the guard at Panchevsky Institute who was on his payroll and discover what could be worked out, and Mrs. Bemish had promised to alert the four Bulgarian prisoners to the possibility of rescue, and try to learn more about the third floor that housed Philip's cell.

The attack on Panchevsky Institute had been set for three o'clock Sunday morning, just before dawn.

On this note they parted, each of them with a sense of astonishment at the events of the evening.

20

The next morning Nevena strode into the lobby of the Rila exuding cheerfulness. "The bus is outside filled with peoples," she told Mrs. Pollifax. "Very nice peoples, all western Europeans. You like Slavko yesterday? You like goose farm? Please recall at seven tonight I come and take you to airport for nine o'clock plane."

"I recall," said Mrs. Pollifax meekly.

"You come now for tour of Sofia."

It was the beginning of a long day, thought Mrs. Pollifax as she seated herself on the Balkantourist bus. It was a luxurious vehicle, with a driver who spoke no English, a small chair beside him for Nevena and a microphone into which she spoke. If Mrs. Pollifax had expected to be bored by Nevena's deluxe tour, she was soon pleasantly surprised.

All along the boulevards flags were flying in the breeze. "You see Sofia in unique moment," announced Nevena, breathing heavily into the microphone, her eyes sparkling. "Tomorrow Comrade Brezhnev, Party Chairman of our great Soviet comrades, come to visit with our leaders. There will be procession and many talks spoken here."

The bus drew to a halt before the National Assembly building so they might observe the wooden stands, the workers installing microphones. "Across, down avenue, consider Georgi Dimitrov Mausoleum," she continued. "There will be ceremony there, too, in morning, the Changing of the Guard for Chairman Brezhnev."

As the tour progressed, Mrs. Pollifax noticed that Nevena showed a definite preference for the new and the Soviet-inspired. Not for her St. George's Church, which had been built in the third century; she was visibly bored. She allowed them an hour to examine the ikons and the Thracian exhibits in the crypt of the Nevsky Cathedral, but plainly what impressed her most was the number of people who came to Bulgaria to see them. However, about the Monument to the Red Army she waxed poetic, and her voice fairly sang as she pointed out the new Pliska and Rila hotels and the apartment complexes on the outskirts of the city. Apparently Nevena was not one of the young people about whom Tsanko worried. Over thirty, probably, thought Mrs. Pollifax.

In the middle of the day they lunched on Mount Vitosha, at the restaurant where Mrs. Pollifax had first learned of Philip's arrest. They descended the mountain in cable cars and met the Balkantourist bus at the bottom, and were whisked off to Boyana to see the church's medieval art. At half-past two Mrs. Pollifax was deposited back at her hotel. "I shall do a little shopping for souvenirs now," she told Nevena reassuringly. "At the Tzum department store."

"But at seven o'clock be in lobby, please," instructed Nevena.

"Yes," said Mrs. Pollifax, and made her way around the corner and down the street to the Tzum, where she confounded the clerks by purchasing nine watches. Following this she spent an hour in her room setting and checking the watches and then on impulse she brought out a stamped postcard and wrote to her neighbor Miss Hartshorne, *Dear Grace, If I should be late in returning—detained for any reason* (such as going to either prison or the firing squad, she thought) *please deliver my night-blooming cereus to Professor Whitsun.* This sounded pessimistic and so she added with a flourish, *Having lovely time, Emily.* And then she tore the postcard up and dropped it into the wastebasket.

At half-past four she put the watches carefully back into the paper shopping bag, locked the door behind her and went downstairs through the lobby to the front entrance. Presently the familiar blue car drew up, she climbed inside and she and Georgi drove away.

The hut in the country had once been a stone house with a thatch roof until a fire had destroyed the roof and blackened the interior. Timbers leaned crazily against the stone walls and sunflowers had begun to weave a new roof of vines. It was charming and pastoral. Above all it was hidden from sight at the edge of a wood and isolated from the nearest tiny village.

"But where is everyone?" asked Mrs. Pollifax as Georgi parked the car under a linden tree.

"Ah, Boris is in the forest rehearsing his fifty-pound hunting bow. You know—he is good, very good? Volko and Radev are in hole under house packing explosives."

"And Debby? Tsanko?"

"Tsanko come to us later. Debby? She is no doubt with Boris rehearsing ropes." He added proudly, "We have long, long rope, very strong, used by men to clean windows very high."

"Scaffolding rope?" suggested Mrs. Pollifax. "I wonder how you found *that.*"

Georgi said eagerly, "You must not think small of our group. Is true Volko and Tsanko and Boris are not young, but they much knowledge, much history. I myself enjoyed much cynicism in beginning, wanting only young people. Now I am different. We join together like sky and clouds, you know? They see the way to get things, they have great knowledge."

Experienced scavengers, thought Mrs. Pollifax with a smile.

"Radev has visited guard he knows. He was gone long time. He brings news this guard Miroslav will go on wall midnight to dawn. At 3 A.M. sharp this man will stop at gate to smoke cigarette and talk. He will not be on wall. But Radev pay much money—oh, wow!"

"Oh, wow?" Mrs. Pollifax laughed. "You've been with Debby!"

"You see that?" he said, grinning. "She is good girl, we become friends today."

"And Mrs. Bemish? Has anyone seen her today?"

"Da. As liaison I go visit her 8 A.M. this morning. She observe and make pictures of windows on Trenda side of Institute. Radev and Boris go over these very very slowly."

"So all the equipment, and all the information, is here," said Mrs. Pollifax as they walked from car to hut.

Georgi nodded. "We gain much experience for Underground. Come—inside."

"I'm curious, Georgi," she said. "You're very young. Why do *you* do all this?"

Georgi looked surprised. "They not tell you? My brother is one of prisoners in Panchevsky."

"Oh—I'm sorry."

"Life imprisonment," said Georgi, nodding. "He is good communist, too, but he disagree with wrong party official, they search apartment and find notebook in which he records the correctness of our becoming freer, like Yugoslavia. They say this very bad, very revisionist." He sighed. "He will not want to leave his beloved Bulgaria, but if he go—maybe things change a little in five, ten years, and he return. Already my country is better now than before. No more—how you call it—bloodlettings? Purges?"

They descended a ladder into the cellar under the house. It was very primitive, no more than a large hole dug out of the earth for storing food. A few scorched herbs still hung from the ceiling. Under them Volko and Radev were checking off small shapeless packages like two earnest storekeepers taking inventory.

"Ah, Amerikanski," said Volko, turning to smile at her. "Welcome! Come see what is done today."

"I'd love to!"

"This Radev is very expert. Radev, tell her."

"Not bad," acknowledged Radev. "Here is ingenious short fuse, two minutes. This is for Tsanko, very powerful, but in small package, you see? We test two of these, they are so perfect maybe I go into business." He grinned. "Here you see six gentler packages of explosive, also for pockets, almost no fuse, maybe five seconds. Two of them delivered today to Mrs. Bemish, two for you and me, four for Georgi and Kosta."

"And the largest one?" she asked.

"Already it is wired to inside of truck. Heaven preserve the accidents, it is to go off with contact."

Mrs. Pollifax drew a deep sigh of relief. "Well, then," she said, looking around her, "everything appears to be going splendidly." She beamed at them. She supposed that guns would have made their plan simpler; Tsanko's hunting rifles had remained in Tarnovo and only Radev had a gun. She had expressed the hope that this would be a nonviolent raid, to which Boris had drawled, "For them or us?" "Both," she'd replied, and he had snorted derisively.

At seven o'clock Volko quietly left—no one explained why—and Georgi spread a large square of cloth on the floor of the hut. There they ate dinner, literally breaking bread together from a huge loaf and washing it down with red wine. Across the tablecloth Debby caught her eye and said, "Isn't this great, Mrs. Pollifax?" She was eating with her fingers, her face healthily pink from the sun. There was nothing waif-like about her today. She's using herself, she's needed, thought Mrs. Pollifax, and wondered why so many people insisted upon happiness being a matter of ease.

Tsanko had still not arrived. "He and Volko go to big gathering," Boris explained when she inquired about them both. "What you call party?"

"Party!" It seemed a most extraordinary time to go partying.

"We decide today—you are not here—that Volko not be with us tonight. We insist he preserve himself because he supply truck and explosives and needs the good story."

"An alibi!" supplied Mrs. Pollifax.

"*Da.* Already he risk much. The police will learn in time where truck come from and they will be harsh. We have arranged for warehouse to be attacked, the locks broken, wooden boxes entered. By who nobody will know, but when they speak with Volko he will be very innocent. All night he will be at ceremony. Given," he added with a grin, "for General Ignatov."

Mrs. Pollifax laughed. "How clever of you all!"

"*Da.* How can head of security doubt the man who drinks with him, eh?" He glanced at his watch. "But Tsanko be here by midnight. You are nervous, Amerikanski?"

"Very," she said.

He nodded. "None of us know, eh? One asks, is this to be died for?"

"And what's your answer?" asked Mrs. Pollifax.

He smiled. "Is not worth dying for, no, but worth being alive to do."

She nodded. "I like you, Boris. I like your skepticism, too."

He shrugged, amused. "It keeps me alive, it entertains me. One must have entertainments, eh?"

It grew slowly dark, and then cold. They could show no lights except in the cellar and after an hour Mrs. Pollifax felt stifled by the smallness of the room and by the single candle that illuminated them. Debby and Georgi talked earnestly in one corner about their countries and their friends. Kosta, Boris and Radev were arguing heatedly in Bulgarian. Watching them, Mrs. Pollifax had too much time to recall her rashnesses, and the many people she had involved in this assault on the Institute, as well as the terrible risks they would all be taking before dawn. Yet given just one small opportunity to save a human life—and the factor of being in the right place at the right time—was there anything to do except try? One made a decision with the mind, she thought—with the cool logic of a chess player—and then it became necessary to grow to it, to curb the emotional protests, resist the longing to give up, to doubt, to flee. The real enemy was fear.

"I believe I shall go out and sit under a tree," she told them.

"Don't go far," Debby called to her.

She was seated under the tree when Tsanko arrived, driving the van without lights across the untilled earth. He did not see her until she called out to him. He walked over and sat down beside her on the rough bench. "It is gravest concern to me how you are tonight," he said. "You are well?"

"Anxious but well," she said.

He nodded. In the darkness his face was dim, without dimension. "No moon, we are fortunate," he said.

They sat quietly together, the sounds of the night encircling them: the shrilling of cicadas, the call of a whippoorwill, a murmur of rustling leaves from the forest. It was extraordinary how fond she had become of this man, thought Mrs. Pollifax, and she reflected upon how few persons there were with whom she felt an instinctive rapport. There was never anything tangible about this. It was composed of humor, attitude, spirit—all invisible —and it made words completely unnecessary between them.

He said abruptly, "You have good life in America? Tell me of this. A *Cpeda*—Wednesday—for instance. What do you do on a Wednesday?"

"Wednesday," repeated Mrs. Pollifax thoughtfully. "I wake up in my apartment in New Brunswick, New Jersey —I have one bedroom, one large, sunny living room and a kitchen with dining space. The New York *Times* is on my doorstep and I read it with my breakfast." It seemed incredibly far away and unreal. "On Wednesdays I wheel the bookcart at the hospital. It's a very *quiet* life," she admitted. "Except on Fridays when I have my karate lessons. And lately I've considered flying lessons."

He looked at her, smiling. "For you this would be good, very good."

"And I have grown a night-blooming cereus on my fire escape," she added almost shyly.

He said quietly, "This is important. Why?"

She hesitated. "Because lately I've had the feeling we rush toward something—some kind of Armageddon—set into motion long ago. There are so many people in the world, and so much destructiveness. I was astonished when I first heard that a night-blooming cereus blooms only once a year, and always at midnight. It implies such *intelligence* somewhere."

"And did it bloom?" he asked.

She nodded triumphantly. "At twenty minutes before midnight, the week before I left for your country."

"Then there are still mysteries left in this world," he said with relief.

"And your Wednesdays?" she asked. "I'm not allowed to ask about your Wednesdays? This is not a dialogue?"

He sighed heavily. "I wish you may, but no, I cannot,

even to you. This is sad because you have become very dear to me, Amerikanski."

She said softly, "It's like a problem in mathematics, I think. For me so much has been added by knowing you, and when I leave–if I am so fortunate," she added wryly, "it will be with a sense of loss, of subtraction."

"At such an age," mused Tsanko, and chuckled. "As if the affections count years! But for me there has been a long time without feeling. My first wife and my little daughter die in 1928–no, not die, they are shot against the wall by the Orim. Murdered. There were three thousand people killed that night, arrested as suspected communists. My daughter had high fever, you see, and despite curfew Adriana wrapped our child in blankets and hurried to find doctor." He shook his head. "My son survived, he is forty now. It was madness, we were not even communists then, But it made one of me," he added.

"How terrible that must have been for you."

"It was. Later I married again, when my son, Vasil, was a grown man–1945, that was. I was most political, and my wife was also political." He shrugged. "That was bad mistake, we have been divorced many years, she is an engineer in Varna. Alas, the climate of Bulgaria is not good for love. But good for peaches," he added with humor, bringing a peach from his pocket. "Please? For you."

They sat eating peaches until Georgi came to the door and said, "There you are–it's time to begin preparing for Panchevsky Institute."

"Suddenly the clock moves too fast," mused Tsanko. "Early in morning I have appointment I cannot avoid. I will not see you again. Everything has been said but this –please do not be killed tonight, Amerikanski."

"Nor you, Tsanko," she said, and they stood silently together for a moment.

"We are of different cultures on the outside," he said slowly, "but inside we are alike. If only you were born

Bulgarian, Amerikanski, we could change the world! You will remember, eh?"

"On Wednesdays," said Mrs. Pollifax gravely.

He laughed. "On Wednesdays, yes," he said, and very formally leaned over and kissed her on each cheek.

21

It was dark and silent in the vicinity of Panchevsky Institute. Only the building itself glowed with light. At five minutes before three o'clock Mrs. Pollifax sat in Assen Radev's farm truck that was filled with honking geese in the rear. She was wearing a shapeless cotton dress, a shabby sweater and over her head a bandanna tied at the nape of her neck. On her shoulder was pinned a card bearing unintelligible letters that supposedly read: I AM A MUTE. "Well, Mrs. Pollifax?" said Radev cheerfully.

She was not quite so cheerful, but she guessed that he was a man who thrived on danger, and therefore his interest in life increased in proportion to the nearness of death. On the whole it was not a bad way to approach Panchevsky Institute, she thought. She glanced at her watch; Radev glanced at his and nodded. "We go," he said, and headed the truck down the street and around the corner into Ordrin Square. Ahead of them, a block away, she could see the walls and the front gate of Panchevsky Institute.

At the top of the hill on Persenk Boulevard, Georgi checked his watch. "One minute to go," he said to Kosta in Bulgarian. "You think we come out of this alive, comrade?"

"Who knows?" said Kosta with a shrug. "It's better to be all dead than half dead."

On the opposite side of the wall, on narrow Ordrin Street, Debby sat beside Boris in the van and shivered from cold and nervousness. "I feel a little sick," she told Boris.

He said very gently, "It's the waiting, you understand. It grows better when there is something to do, you will see."

"It's one minute before three o'clock, Boris," she said, looking at her watch. He nodded, climbed out and began to unlock the rear door of the van where the ladder was hidden.

Tsanko had crossed Persenk Boulevard and now he strolled along beside the high wall, one hand in his pocket fingering the bundle there. Reaching the middle of the wall, he checked his watch, kneeled as if to tie a shoelace and inserted the bundle tightly against the wall. A match flared. When he straightened he began to walk very swiftly, almost running toward a van parked diagonally across the road, near Stalinov Avenue. He appeared not to notice the large truck soundlessly moving toward him down Persenk Boulevard on his left; it gained momentum as it neared the bottom of the hill. Tsanko had just opened the door to the van when the outer wall of Panchevsky Institute erupted, a portion of it bursting into fragments. The sound of the explosion followed a second later, just as the massive truck rolled through the broken wall and entered the courtyard.

Half a minute later came the sound of the truck's crash, followed by a second, louder explosion.

At the gate Assen Radev was saying, "You may not be expecting two dozen geese for your kitchens, but they are your dinner today. Hell, what do you want done with them? Who's in charge? I tell you they are ordered for this morning."

The guard pointed to Mrs. Pollifax, and Radev said carelessly, "She belongs at the collective, I'm taking her back. She can't speak, she's a mute."

A second man casually joined them and with a wink at Radev spoke persuasively to his companion; it was Miroslav, earning his bribe. The guard fingered the papers with annoying slowness and then nodded. "Take them into the inside court, they can kill the geese there, idiot. But be fast."

Slowly the truck from the collective inched through the gates and then through the second iron gate into the courtyard. "You see the stairs?" said Radev in a low voice to Mrs. Pollifax. "On the right. The door to each floor is kept locked, but the stairs are clear and go up to the top floor."

Mrs. Pollifax nodded. She climbed out and opened the tailgate at the back of the truck. Two dozen geese stared at her, and with a furious motion she gestured them outside, scattering them as they fluttered to the ground honking in outrage. A moment later came the sound of the first explosion.

Boris and Debby heard the sound of the first explosion as they waited in Ordrin Street, the ladder half out of the van. It was dark on the street, but noonday on the top of the wall, and Debby was thinking about Mrs. Bemish and the lights. If Mrs. Bemish couldn't reach them —or damaged them too late—what on earth could they do?

"Set up the ladder," Boris told her. "I'll go first and

you follow. Watch the ropes—nothing must tangle them! Do it as we practiced all day."

"I will."

They heard the second explosion and then, abruptly, the sound of a siren began to shrill and was just as suddenly cut off as the lights all over the Institute died. Mrs. Bemish had reached the fuse box. "Now," said Boris, and they hurried up the ladder.

Georgi and Kosta were bent low in the truck as it rolled through the gaping hole in the outer wall and continued, on momentum alone, through the Institute courtyard. As it neared the brick wall of the Institute, Georgi shouted, "Jump, my friend!"

They threw themselves out of the truck, rolling over and over until they crouched under the walls of the building. The truck roared through the wall, setting off the explosives wired under its hood; bricks and stones rained down all around them. "Now," shouted Georgi, and they leaped over the rubble and ran into the cellblock. They were hailed by cheers from the cells and Georgi was grinning as he made his way through the dust. There was plenty of dynamite, he was thinking. He would first free their four friends, among them his brother, but while Kosta hurried the four out to Tsanko there would be time to release a few others as well. They might not get far, but what the hell, he thought; they could have a taste of freedom, smell the free air, feel like men again. He could give them choice at least.

He was opening the door of his brother's cell when the lights went out.

In the inner courtyard Radev and Mrs. Pollifax were busy directing the geese consistently toward the stairs leading up into the higher cellblocks. Before the echo of the first explosion had died away at least six of the frightened geese had settled on the stair. As the second explosion took place Mrs. Pollifax and Radev each seized a goose and ran up the stairs, driving the dozen others before them. They had reached the second-floor landing when the lights went out. Someone came running down the staircase, tripped over the geese and brushed past Mrs. Pollifax with an oath. With the goose under her arm Mrs. Pollifax continued to climb. A dark shape suddenly careened into her, almost knocking her over; a man grasped her arm, a match flared, a guard spoke sharply and Mrs. Pollifax lifted the goose, making noises in her throat and pointing skyward. The guard disgustedly gestured her aside, blew out the match and hurried on down the stairs.

She had lost Radev; the goose she carried had just learned that by arching his long neck he could peck at her chin and draw blood. With considerable relief Mrs. Pollifax reached the third floor and paused. The door stood open, knocked from its hinges, and she could hear the fluttering of wings ahead of her in the darkness.

She went in quietly, disoriented and suddenly without direction. She faced a long dark hall with a window at the far end; to her left lay another window. Between these stood cellblocks, line after line of them. She stood there, lost until a light flared at the window on her left. The light sputtered like a Fourth of July sparkler, made a small sound and then she saw Radev lean forward, silhouetted against the sky, and lift out the bars of the window. She dropped the goose and joined him just in time to help him pick up the rope Boris had shot across the yard and secure it to the bars of a cell.

Geese were honking. All over the building men were shouting. She called out, "Philip? Philip Trenda?"

"I have to be dreaming," said an American voice from the cell next to the window.

"Over here," she told Radev, and he lighted a match. In its glow they saw a white face with hollow eyes staring at them from behind bars, a face Mrs. Pollifax had last seen at Customs, on Monday. She said inadequately, tears in her eyes, "Hello there," and then: "We've come to get you out."

Debby kneeled on the wall next to Boris, her teeth chattering. Once in a while they had gently tested the rope, but it remained slack and without support. It was awful, waiting, thought Debby. She tried to picture Mrs. Pollifax and Radev climbing the stairs to the third floor, tried to live it with them. She wished she could have gone with Radev; Tsanko had said no, a pretty young girl would draw too much attention at the gate.

They ought to be there now, she thought, and staring at the window she was rewarded by the sight of a small flicker of light. She whispered to Boris, "They've reached the window."

Crouched low, Boris said, *"Da,* thank God!" He leaned over and tested the rope, tugging gently. Triumphantly he said, "It is anchored, we get ready now. Say your prayers!"

Now Mrs. Pollifax and Radev would have found Phil, the last bundle of dynamite would be applied to the lock of his cell and any moment he would be at the window, ready to cross. "How much more time?" she asked Boris.

He glanced down at his illuminated watch. "It is now 3:11."

"He ought to be crossing," she whispered. "Radev and Mrs. Pollifax ought to be going downstairs to the truck."

"Patience," said Boris.

Debby strained her eyes trying to peer through the darkness. She leaned over and felt the rope; it was secure, but there was no weight on it. She thought, I won't panic, but he ought to be crossing. I'm not scared, I'm not. She realized that never before had she cared or felt so much about two people as she did at this moment. It was insane, it was as though her whole life had begun only a week ago. She was suddenly terrified for everyone involved in this, but she was the most frightened for Phil and Mrs. Pollifax.

"Boris," she said, her voice trembling.

He turned and she saw him nod. "*Da*—something is wrong," he said heavily.

"I know," she said, and stood up.

On the third floor of the Institute, Radev had stuffed dynamite into the lock of Philip's cell and applied a match to it. As the light flared for a brief second Philip Trenda said to Mrs. Pollifax in astonishment, "I've seen you before! I know I've seen you before!"

"Ssh," hissed Radev.

The fuse ignited and Mrs. Pollifax stepped back. There was the sound of a muffled *crack!* and they were in darkness again, but in that darkness Mrs. Pollifax felt someone breathing down her neck from behind. She said in a low voice, "Assen?"

But Radev was opening the door of the cell. She said, "Who . . . ?" but before she could turn around she felt a gun pressed into the small of her back.

Radev had not noticed. The person behind Mrs. Pollifax suddenly spoke to Radev roughly, in Bulgarian, and Radev growled in his throat and turned.

"What is it?" asked Mrs. Pollifax. "Who is it?"

"It's Miroslav, the guard."

"He has a gun in my back," protested Mrs. Pollifax.

Radev spoke sharply to the man and the gun was removed. In the darkness Miroslav and Radev shifted positions cautiously. Miroslav backed to the window to stand outlined against it, gun in hand. Radev moved away from Philip's cell in order to conceal the rope tied to its bars. They stood like this in silence and then Radev spoke to the man in anger.

It was torture not knowing what they said. Radev's voice was biting; Miroslav's was calm. The man had been well paid—and not even in counterfeit rubles, after all, but in authentic Bulgarian *leva*—but still he stood with his gun directed at them, not willing to let them go. "What *is* it?" cried Mrs. Pollifax impatiently.

"The dog," said Radev, and spat on the floor. "The *dog*. He took the bribe, now he says he gets more money turning us in and getting a medal. He didn't know I was going to release the American capitalist spy."

Mrs. Pollifax heard Philip say, "Oh God."

"He's barricading the window," went on Radev, "and he says in a few minutes both lights and guards will return. He has only to wait."

"Does he speak English?"

"No."

"Have you any dynamite left?"

"No."

"He hasn't noticed the rope yet. If one of us could just reach him and hold him long enough for Philip to get to the window . . ."

Radev's voice was cynical. "You wish to volunteer? That's exactly what he's waiting for." Then in a peculiar voice he added, "Wait. Something is happening."

"What?" demanded Mrs. Pollifax.

"Ssh," he said, and then: "Pray God the lights do not come on. The rope is tight, do you understand?"

"Tight," echoed Mrs. Pollifax uncomprehendingly and then she realized that in concealing the rope Radev stood where he could also touch it, and her heart began to beat very fast. "Talk to him," she said in a low voice. "Keep him talking, Radev."

"*Da.*"

Mrs. Pollifax fixed her eyes on the barless window behind Miroslav. She saw a hand grasp the window sill and then the silhouette of a slim body drag itself up to the sill. In a clear conversational voice Mrs. Pollifax addressed the shadow. "The guard stands with a gun, and with his back to the window. *His back to the window!*"

The figure was crouched there now, black against the sky. It was Debby.

Tackle, she thought silently. Tackle, Debby, *tackle!*

Debby stood up, remained poised for a second on the sill and then hurled herself toward the floor of the cellblock, taking Miroslav with her. With trembling fingers Mrs. Pollifax lighted a match. It was enough for Radev; he found Miroslav, bent over him and wrested the gun from his hands. A moment later Debby stood up. Behind her there was the sound of bone hitting bone, a groan and then Radev said, "He's out cold."

"Debby—oh thank God you made it," gasped Mrs. Pollifax.

"Debby?" repeated Philip incredulously. "Debby's here?"

"I'm here," Debby said in a steady voice. "Phil, there's a rope attached to the window and you have to go quickly, hand over hand, so that the rest of us can follow. Can you?"

"With pleasure," he said fervently.

Radev said, "We can't all go by rope, there isn't time. I have Miroslav's gun. How about it, Mrs. Pollifax? Shall we make a fast retreat by the stairs into hell knows what?"

"Yes," said Mrs. Pollifax. She reached out, grasped Debby's hand and squeezed it. "You won't wait too long?"

"I won't," promised Debby.

Mrs. Pollifax and Radev walked down the hall to the staircase. A goose rushed at them and Radev scooped it up and pushed it into Mrs. Pollifax's arms. They descended as quickly as they dared in the darkness, braced for discovery at any minute. They reached the last landing and then the inner courtyard and now they saw why they had not been challenged yet: fires had broken out following the explosions and the courtyard was filled with black smoke. They jumped into the truck and Radev backed and turned it and they drove through the first gate. At the second gate Radev called out to the solitary guard at the sentry box.

The guard came running. To Mrs. Pollifax's surprise Radev cut the guard's questions short with a laugh reached over and took the goose from her and tossed it into the man's arms. A moment later the guard opened the gates for them.

"He wanted only to ask about the fire," said Radev. "I told him he will have roast geese for dinner."

As they drove through the gates the lights and the siren of Panchevsky Institute came on simultaneously. Mrs. Pollifax looked down at her watch: it was precisely 3:27. She said blankly, "It's over. It's over, Radev, and we're still alive!"

"Beginner's luck, eh, Comrade Pollifax?" said Radev.

Minutes later they reached the appointed rendezvous in a park at the edge of Sofia, and what was most satisfying of all, Debby and Boris and Philip were in the car behind them.

22

Outside the Hotel Rila a man was sweeping the street with a broom of thick twigs tied around a crooked stick. The sky brightened during the past hour and there was a suffusion of pink in the east where the sun was rising. As Mrs. Pollifax mounted the steps of the hotel she turned and saw Georgi and the small blue car disappear for the last time and then she entered the lobby, properly dressed as a tourist again, her purse over her arm. A dozing desk clerk jerked awake and stared at her reproachfully. She wrote the number of her room on his memo pad and he handed her the key. He also handed over her passport, which had been placed in the box, and she tucked it into her purse.

As she ascended in the elevator to the sixth floor she felt a sense of sadness. It was completely illogical, she reminded herself, because the sacking of Panchevsky Institute had been accomplished without bloodshed and with a success beyond all expectation. What was more, the passports she had delivered to Tsanko were about to save five lives as well as give new lives to Mrs. Bemish and Assen Radev.

I'm just very tired, she thought.

She tried to remember that she and Debby, Philip and Mrs. Bemish would be meeting on Monday in Zurich, in front of the bank to which Petrov Trendafilov would bring the ransom, but even this didn't lift her sagging spirits.

She tried also to remember Philip's astonishment at meeting her again, or the flash of Assen Radev's grin as he said, "Beginner's luck, eh, Comrade Pollifax?" But another voice blotted them out, a voice that she would remember the rest of her life: *I am not sure either of us is professional, is this not so? . . . I am good communist, a patriot and also—God help me—a humanist. . . . You have become very dear to me, Amerikanski.*

The elevator opened at the sixth floor and she walked down the hall to her room and inserted the key into the lock. She already missed Debby, but Debby would be making her way to the airport alone after she had helped to change Philip into Anton Schoenstein, a German with German credentials and clothes. She opened the door and flicked on the lights and brought her suitcase from the closet and carried it to the bed. Moving to the bureau, she picked up comb, brush and cold cream. She glanced at herself in the mirror and was startled to see how little changed she looked after twenty-seven minutes inside Panchevsky Institute. Perhaps one day next year—very suddenly—new lines would etch themselves on her face and she could say, *Those are Panchevsky lines.*

Suddenly in the mirror she saw the door to the bathroom open silently. A foot—a black boot—inserted itself against the door and Nikolai Dzhagarov moved into the doorway and stood watching her. Their glances met in the mirror.

"You have perhaps forgotten me," he said, bringing out a gun. "My name is Nikki."

"Yes, I *had* forgotten you," she admitted. "Foolishly," she added in a low voice.

"You may turn around now—slowly, hands up," he said. "You will forget the suitcase, Mrs. Pollifax, you are my prisoner and before I let you go I must know how to find my friend Debby and my friend Carleton Bemish."

Slowly Mrs. Pollifax turned, hands lifted.

"Now. First you will tell me where Karlo Bemish and Titko Yugov are to be found."

Mrs. Pollifax's first reaction was one of relief: Nikki was still twenty-four hours behind them, he didn't know about the prison raid, his mind was stubbornly fixed on Tarnovo, which felt to her like a century ago. Her second reaction was the more realistic. Dzhagarov had all the time in the world, and a gun, and he was a dangerous man. She might have to die tonight.

"I didn't think you cared about Mr. Bemish," she said lightly. "You certainly exploited him rather cruelly, didn't you?"

Nikki shrugged. "He asked for it. What a bore, that man, always talking of his millionaire brother-in-law in America! An obsession. When he learned Phil would be visiting Yugoslavia in July he had the audacity to try and bribe me so that he might go to Belgrade and collect a few dollars from the boy." He laughed savagely. "A few thousand was all he wanted, can you imagine? What a small mind!"

"I wonder if I might lower my hands," said Mrs. Pollifax hopefully.

"No." He left the doorway and moved across the room toward her. As he passed the bed he reached out and shoved her suitcase to the floor, kicking it viciously across the room. "So much for your departure," he said contemptuously. "I want to know where Bemish can be found. I want to know where Debby is. She's been in

Bulgaria all this time, she did not leave with the others. Why?"

"Debby left Bulgaria last night," she told him. "If you ask at the desk you'll discover she picked up her passport late yesterday afternoon. She's gone."

"No one by that name flew out of Sofia yesterday or last night or early this morning. She is still here." He moved behind her and placed the point of his pistol at the back of her neck. It felt cold against her flesh. "Where is she?"

"I don't know," said Mrs. Pollifax.

"Where is Bemish?"

"I don't know," repeated Mrs. Pollifax.

The pistol burrowed deeper. "I will count to four," he said. "If you do not speak I will kill you."

"Yes," she said numbly.

"One," said Nikki.

Mrs. Pollifax closed her eyes. She remembered that Tsanko was safe and that he had taken to safety the four men who had been rescued. The four would presently be leaving Bulgaria by bus, car and boat. Assen Radev had been given his well-earned passport and perhaps—knowing Radev—was already across the border.

"Two," said Nikki.

But they all needed time, she thought: Debby and Philip, especially.

"Try Bemish first," suggested Nikki smoothly. "You were in Tarnovo that same night he disappeared. You saw him—of course you saw him."

She shook her head. "I didn't see him."

"Three," said Nikki, and waited.

Mrs. Pollifax also waited. It would be a sudden and clean death, she thought, and she had always known the odds were against her dying in bed at home in New Brunswick, New Jersey.

Suddenly Nikki laughed and removed the gun from her neck. "You have strong nerves. You think I kill you so quickly—here of all places—without learning what I wish to know? Pick up the suitcase on the floor and close it."

Mrs. Pollifax sighed, crossed the room and placed the suitcase on the bed.

"Put the coat on and pick up the purse," he directed. When she had done this he added, "Now carry the suitcase out the door ahead of me. You will proceed down the hall to the elevator, then to the lobby, out of the lobby to my car. Walk!"

She picked up the empty suitcase and went to the door. "Where are we going?" she asked quietly.

"Headquarters. They will know how to deal with you there. The new head of security, General Ignatov, will see that you talk—he knows all the ways. Don't turn around!" he said sharply. "I shall be directly behind you, gun in pocket."

Mrs. Pollifax walked steadily down the hall to the elevator. If there was a long wait for the elevator, she thought, it might be possible to draw close enough to Dzhagarov to catch him off balance with a kick and a shin strike.

Unfortunately the elevator was standing at the sixth floor, depressingly empty, its doors wide open.

"In," said Nikki, and joined her only when she had walked to the rear.

They descended, facing each other. When the elevator stopped he said, "Walk out now. Speak to no one and cross the lobby. A car is outside, the safety catch is off my gun. No tricks."

The doors of the elevator slid open and Mrs. Pollifax walked out into the lobby. She realized that she was about to enter a Bulgaria that no tourists were allowed to see, and the lobby was her last glimpse of the familiar.

"So there you are, Mrs. Pollifax!" cried an indignant and familiar voice. Nevena stood beside the desk, hands on hips. "How insulting you are, Mrs. Pollifax! I am here at 7 P.M. sharp last night and you are not here, now they call from the hotel to say you are back, and again I must leave my work to find you! *Bora!* It is too much."

Mrs. Pollifax stopped uncertainly, the gun at her back.

"You have your suitcase—good," continued Nevena, walking toward her. "They tell me you have been given passport as well. You will come at once, please, this is gravest dishonor for you. Yes, yes, what is it, Comrade Dzhagarov?" she asked impatiently.

"She is mine," Nikki told her coldly, and began speaking to her rapidly in Bulgarian.

"Nonsense—she is mine," Nevena interrupted sharply. "Speak in English, Comrade Dzhagarov, or you will make the scandal. People are listening, you understand? This woman is not yours, she is to leave country at once, she is *persona non grata*. Balkantourist is *finis* with her. Kaput!"

Nikki said icily, "I tell you she is mine, Comrade Chernokolev. I have orders she must go to headquarters for interrogation."

"Show me the orders," Nevena said angrily.

Nikki shrugged. "They are not written. You wish to cross General Ignatov?"

"General Ignatov!" Nevena laughed. "Idiot—he was arrested only a few hours ago. By now he is on his way to Panchevsky Institute."

"Arrested?" repeated Nikki. "I do not believe you. What a liar you are!"

She shrugged. "Please yourself, comrade, but you would do well not to speak his name. I will be kind and forget you spoke of him."

Nikki looked shaken. "This is not possible. On what charges?"

Nevena looked at him scornfully. "His home is searched last night while he is at celebration. Big fortune in Russian rubles is found there."

"So?"

"The rubles were counterfeit," Nevena said curtly, and

grasping Mrs. Pollifax firmly by the arm she led her out of the door to a waiting car.

"You see the trouble you make," Nevena continued as she pushed her into the car. "It is Sunday, I do not work on Sunday." She started the motor and they hurtled forward. "I anticipate viewing of Party Chairman Brezhnev's arrival from Moscow and now you make the work for me, *more* work."

Mrs. Pollifax turned her head and looked at her wordlessly.

"They already begin the ropes along the street," went on Nevena hotly, "and I doubt gravely we get to aerodrome in time for the early plane to Belgrade. Soon they stop cars."

"Yes," said Mrs. Pollifax, testing her voice and surprised to find that she could still speak.

"Dzhagarov is arrogant," said Nevena. "As for you, Mrs. Pollifax—please. You are too old for travel. Go home to your children, your grandchildren, you understand?"

Mrs. Pollifax drew a deep breath; it was beginning to dawn upon her that she was going to survive this day, after all. The cool, early morning air was reviving her; it occurred to her that she had been very near to a state of collapse back at the hotel. She realized that Nevena had no idea at all that she had just saved her life, and this struck her as incredible and wonderful and a little hilarious, and this, too, revived her. "Yes," she said to Nevena, and her eyes turned to Mount Vitosha and then to the sun spilling gold across the road and to the clusters of vivid blue asters.

"Do me the favor of staying in your home," went on Nevena, driving very fast, her profile stern. "You have not the gift of coordination."

"No," Mrs. Pollifax said humbly.

Nevena swerved to avoid a flock of sheep crossing the road. *"Nahot,"* she said under her breath, and sent the car racing down still another country road. "You Americans must learn the purpose, the punctualness. I forgive much because you are old, but never come back to my country, you understand?"

"I understand," said Mrs. Pollifax, clinging to her seat.

They emerged on a broad boulevard. "You see the police collecting," pointed out Nevena reproachfully. "Chairman Brezhnev must already be landing at the aerodrome, we may be cut off. I drive quick, but I do not know. When the glorious leader of the Soviet Union comes to our country it is great honor."

"It's going to be a lovely day," ventured Mrs. Pollifax. "For his arrival," she added quickly as Nevena gave her a suspicious glance.

"We make good time—there is entrance to aerodrome," Nevena announced, and with a quick glance at her watch added, "We have ten minutes to get you to Customs, half an hour to plane departure." But as they began the long drive into the terminal Nevena clucked suddenly and with exasperation. "We are to be stopped," she said.

A barricade had been set up just this side of the terminal, and uniformed police were standing around it. They gestured the car to the side and Nevena handed one of the guards her credentials, speaking vivaciously and pointing ahead. The guard shook his head.

Nevena said with a shrug, "Well, we must stop, but not for long, and it is gravest honor for you, Mrs. Pollifax—you also will observe the Chairman Brezhnev pass by. The procession is just leaving the air terminal." She parked the car and climbed out. "Come if you please," she said indifferently. "For me this is happy moment, I see the Chairman after all."

Mrs. Pollifax climbed out of the car and joined Nevena by the side of the road—it seemed a very small way in which to repay Nevena for saving her life. She stood quietly as the procession of cars slowly approached: first the uniformed men on motorcycles, then one long, black, closed limousine–"There is Chairman Brezhnev with our Premier!" cried Nevena, stiffening in a salute–and following this came three open limousines filled with wooden-faced men in black suits.

How stiff and Slavic they looked, thought Mrs. Pollifax, amused, and then her glance rested upon one of the men in the second limousine and she stared in astonishment. There was no mistaking that profile, that square jaw, those shaggy brows. She said, "Who . . ." and then she stopped and cleared her throat and said, "Who are the men in the cars following your Premier, Nevena?"

"Members of our Politburo." said Nevena, not turning. "High officials of our government."

I have an appointment early in the morning, Tsanko had said.

The heads remained fixed, like statues–he did not see her–and standing behind Nevena, unseen by her, Mrs. Pollifax lifted a hand and gravely saluted, too.

23

It was early Monday morning in Langley Field, Virginia, and just six o'clock as Carstairs entered his office. With the Trenda affair so tragically ended by the boy's death there was a great deal of back work to clear away. It was all very well to begin a day at the leisurely hour of nine if dealing with American affairs, but at that hour in America it was already 2 P.M. in Europe.

As Carstairs sat down at his desk Bishop suddenly appeared in the doorway of the adjacent room, yawning and shaking his head. Carstairs said in astonishment, "Good God, what on earth are you doing here at this hour?"

Bishop peered at him through glazed eyes. "Sleeping. I had a date. Seemed a hell of a lot simpler to come here at four o'clock in the morning than go all the way back to my apartment."

"You look like death itself," Carstairs told him with a shudder. "Go and wash your face and get us some coffee."

"Adrenalin would be better," Bishop said bleakly and went out rubbing his eyes.

Carstairs returned to the pile of reports on his desk from South America, Iraq, Helsinki and Vienna. There was still nothing from Bulgaria and this began to be alarming. He'd sent an urgent message to Assen Radev through emergency channels demanding that Radev track down and recover both Mrs. Pollifax and her coat. That message had gone off four days ago, on Wednesday night, with instructions that its arrival be verified at once —and no verification had come through. He didn't like it, he didn't like any part of the summing up: nothing from Radev since the last routine message reporting the secret police tailing Mrs. Pollifax, and nothing from Mrs. Pollifax, who should have left Bulgaria yesterday, on Sunday.

What did it mean—betrayal? . . . God, it was hard not knowing.

Bishop reappeared carrying a pot of coffee and looking decently shaved and alert again. "Morning," he said cheerfully. "The medical records on young Trenda have just come through from his family doctor." He tossed them on the desk.

"I suppose there's absolutely no history of rheumatic fever or heart deficiency?"

"None at all, sir."

"Just as we thought," said Carstairs gloomily, his eyes scanning the records. "I assume his father will agree to an autopsy as soon as he's brought back the body?"

Bishop hesitated. "I understand not, sir."

"What?" Bishop was shocked and incredulous. "Why the hell not?"

"He left for Europe Saturday night, you know, after refusing to speak to reporters at the airport. Earlier, in Chicago—just after the announcement of his son's death— he said very flatly 'no autopsy.'"

The desk was suddenly too confining for Carstairs and he sprang to his feet and began pacing. "There's something horribly wrong here," he said, "and I'm not seeing where yet."

"About Philip's death, you mean?"

Carstairs brushed this aside impatiently. "Of course about Trenda's death—we can *all* smell the convenience of it, but I doubt that murder can ever be proven. No, I mean there's something horribly wrong about *everything*. Mrs. Pollifax is hell knows where with the secret police tailing her. Radev's silent. And Mr. Trenda says 'no autopsy.' Why? What does he know that we don't? What do they know in Bulgaria that we don't?"

"The telephone, sir."

Carstairs whirled and glared at him, saw the orange light flashing at his desk and swore. "Damn, I came in early to escape telephone calls. All right, acknowledge the blasted thing, Bishop."

Bishop leaned over and flicked off the light. "Carstairs' office, Bishop speaking . . . " He was silent and then he shouted, *"What?"* He swiveled in his chair and signaled Carstairs. "Yes, we certainly *will* accept a collect call from Mrs. Emily Pollifax in Zurich, Switzerland."

Carstairs' jaw dropped. "She's safe? She's calling?" He crossed the room in two strides. "Hello?" he barked into the telephone. "Hello? Connection's not through yet," he growled to Bishop. "Get this on tape, will you? And what the hell's she doing in Switzerland?"

Bishop switched on the tape recorder and took the liberty of plugging in the headset jack and adjusting the headset to his ears. At the other end of the line he heard a familiar voice say, "Mr. Carstairs? Is that you, Mr. Carstairs?"

Bishop grinned. It was extraordinary how lighthearted he suddenly felt.

"Go ahead, please," the overseas operator said.

"Thank God!" cried Carstairs. "You're all right, Mrs. Pollifax?"

"I'm just fine," said Mrs. Pollifax happily. "I hope you are, too? Mr. Carstairs, I realize this is ruinously expensive for the taxpayers, my calling you from Europe—"

"They've borne worse," said Carstairs savagely. "Mrs. Pollifax, we heard the secret police were trailing you. Were you able to meet Tsanko?"

"Oh yes—a marvelous man," she told him warmly. "But I'm not calling about that, I'm calling about a passport. There's a young American student with me who's had his passport confiscated—"

"You say you *did* meet Tsanko," said Carstairs with relief.

"Yes, he has the hat and its contents, Mrs. Carstairs. But you didn't tell me about the coat. Or Assen Radev." Her voice was mildly reproachful.

"Radev?" echoed Carstairs. "You know his name? You met him? That was expressly forbidden, Mrs. Pollifax, I'll have his head for that."

"If you can find him," replied Mrs. Pollifax pleasantly. "He flew out with us yesterday and I hope you'll be kind to him, he was so *very* helpful."

"What do you mean, 'flew out'?" Carstairs said ominously. "He belongs in Bulgaria. He's paid to *stay* in Bulgaria."

"Oh well, he couldn't possibly stay after the trouble began, you know. I think you'll find them on the French Riviera, he said something about a vacation. But Mr. Carstairs, I'm calling about this young American—"

"What trouble?" he demanded. "Mrs. Pollifax, did Radev catch up with your coat and exchange it or didn't he?"

"You mean the counterfeit rubles," said Mrs. Pollifax pleasantly. "No, I don't believe he ever saw them, but in any case it scarcely matters because General Ignatov has them now, and he—"

Carstairs said slowly, "Mrs. Pollifax, I thought I heard you say General Ignatov, but the connection's poor. *Who* has the rubles?"

Mrs. Pollifax sighed. "General Ignatov, but he's gone to prison so that scarcely matters either. Mr. Carstairs

I'm *not* telephoning about Assen Radev or General Ignatov, I'm calling about this young American whose passport was confiscated. It's very important, he wants to return tomorrow and I know that a word from you will restore his passport."

"My dear Mrs. Pollifax," he said irritably, "I can't possibly interfere in such matters, that's strictly State Department business. It's naïve of you even to ask, because you can't be certain at all that he's American."

"But of course he is," said Mrs. Pollifax indignantly. "I entered Bulgaria with him and he was American when he was arrested. Perhaps you've read about him in the newspapers, his name is Philip Trenda."

There was a baffled silence. "Philip Trenda?" repeated Carstairs.

"Yes, you've read about him?"

"Read about him! He's been the major headline for a week. But he's dead, Mrs. Pollifax. He died in Belgrade on Friday."

Mrs. Pollifax sighed. "No, he didn't die, Mrs. Carstairs, that's what I'm trying to explain. He's here in Zurich with me, in fact we're all here at the Grand Hotel, his father, too. It was someone else they sent to Belgrade, and that's why his passport is gone, you see, but we were able to get him out."

"Out?"

"Yes, out of Panchevsky Institute."

"Nonsense," Carstairs said flatly. "Nobody gets out of Panchevsky Institute."

"Well, I'm sorry to disillusion you. We got him out of Panchevsky Institute and then out of Bulgaria."

"And who the hell's we?" demanded Carstairs.

"The Underground. But Philip's traveling under the name of Anton Schoenstein, you see, and since it's one of your forged passports I'm not at all sure that he'll be allowed into the United States, and—"

Carstairs interrupted in a dazed voice. "Miss Pollifax, are you trying to tell me that Philip Trenda's *alive?*"

"Of course," she said cheerfully. "It's why I called, but I do think I must hang up now because they're waiting for me on the balcony. We're having a champagne breakfast, you see, because we're all safe and because the ransom wasn't paid, so if you'll excuse me—"

"Ransom!" shouted Carstairs. "What ransom? Mrs. Pollifax!"

"Yes?"

"I'm taking the next plane over! Don't move from that hotel and don't let Philip Trenda or his father speak to a soul, do you hear? Good God, this sounds like State Department business at the highest level."

He hung up. In a hollow voice he said, "Did you get that on tape, Bishop? Every word?"

"I certainly did, sir. And eavesdropped as well."

"I sent her to Bulgaria to deliver eight passports," Carstairs said, looking stunned. "How in the hell did she end up putting General Ignatov in prison, corrupting our last agent in Sofia and resurrecting a dead American?"

"Definitely a meddler," Bishop said, grinning. "Now shall I call the State Department first or the air lines, sir?"

At the other end of the line, in Zurich, Mrs. Pollifax hung up the telephone, crossed the room and opened the glass doors to the balcony. On the threshold she paused a minute to admire the scene in front of her, the long table heaped with flowers, waiters hovering, the Trendas and Debby seated and waiting for her. A motley group, she thought with a smile. There was Peter Trenda, nee Petrov Trendafilov, a delightful little man with a shock of hair as white as his linen suit. To his right sat Philip, his eyes a shade less haunted today, although his face was still pale and tired. Mrs. Bemish sat on his left, looking already younger and straighter as she beamed at her brother. And there was Debby, her hair swept high on her head today and her eyes like stars.

Survivors of a strange week, thought Mrs. Pollifax.

"Champagne for breakfast!" Debby was saying in an awed voice as the waiter leaned over and filled her glass. "Not to mention breakfast at noon. It's so rococo, like one of those late late movies starring Carole Lombard."

"Well, after all, Dad's sitting here with a million bucks in that attaché case. Hey," Phil said, looking up and seeing Mrs. Pollifax, "come and join us, the party's ready to begin and there's so much to tell Dad. Did your phone call go through?"

Nodding, she crossed the balcony to the table. "Yes, but it was *such* a difficult conversation—Mr. Carstairs didn't seem to have the slightest idea what I was talking about."

Debby laughed. "That's because he hasn't been with you for the past week!"

"He's taking the next plane over," Mrs. Pollifax told Mr. Trenda. "You and Philip aren't to speak to anyone until he arrives. Something about the State Department."

Peter Trenda nodded. "I quite approve. They will not want to embarrass Bulgaria about this. We are both incognito anyway," he added with a smile, "since I am registered here as Petrov Trendafilov, and my son is still Anton Schoenstein. My son," he repeated, smiling at Philip. "My son who is risen from the dead. Mrs. Pollifax . . . Debby . . ." His voice broke. "How can I ever express what I feel this morning when I approach the bank and find you all waiting for me? You have returned to me my son and my sister."

Mrs. Pollifax smiled. Lightly, to cover the emotion of the moment, she said, "I think some toasts are in order, don't you? So much champagne!"

Trenda nodded. "You are very wise—the joy and the tears are very near to us just now. Well, Philip? To you I give the first toast because you are truly the host today."

Philip looked about him at their faces. He said soberly, "All right. I think I'll go back to the beginning of all this and propose a toast to a chance meeting in the Belgrade air terminal. That's where it all began isn't it?"

"But is anything chance, I wonder?" mused Mrs. Pollifax.

Peter Trenda smiled. "You feel that, too?" he asked. Lifting his glass, he said, "Then let us drink next—very seriously—to the arrivals and departures of life, that they may never be careless."

Debby suddenly shivered.

"What is it, Deb?" asked Phil. "Cold?"

"No." There were tears in her eyes. "I don't know, I really don't. Except—for a whole week I've been tired and frightened, I nearly got murdered three times and my thumb was broken and—I've never felt so good. Will you let me make the next toast? If anyone will lend me a handkerchief, that is."

"Handkerchief!" exclaimed Mr. Trenda, laughing. "Please—I would give you my life, young lady, a handkerchief is nothing."

"Thanks," Debby said, and wiped her eyes. Lifting her glass, she stared at it for so long and so thoughtfully that Mrs. Pollifax wondered what she was seeing in its golden contents.

We have each returned a little bemused and enchanted, she thought.

Debby said soberly, "This toast can only be to one person, a very brave man named Tsanko."

Mrs. Pollifax became suddenly still and alert.

"We don't know who he was," she went on with a scowl. "I don't suppose anyone will ever know. But he saved our lives in Tarnovo and we wouldn't be here now if it weren't for him. But also this toast is to him because . . ." She blushed and darted a quick, apologetic glance at Mrs. Pollifax. "Because someday I hope a man will look at me the way he looked at Mrs. Pollifax."

"Hear, hear," said Phil softly.

"I like this girl," Mr. Trenda said, smiling at Mrs. Pollifax. "Shall we drink our next toast to this man, then?"

"To Tsanko," Debby said, nodding. "Whoever he is."

"To Tsanko," echoed Mrs. Pollifax, smiling, and for just a moment—but there would be many such moments —her thoughts traveled back to a moonlit fortress in Tarnovo, to a bench outside a country hut, and from there at last to a procession of passing limousines. *And may no one ever learn who he is,* she added silently, like a prayer.